THE SUNDAY SCHOOL TEACHER II

COLE HART

Cole Hart

Mailing List

To stay up to date on new releases, plus get information on contests, sneak peeks, and more,

Go To The Website Below...

WWW.COLEHARTSIGNATURE.COM

CHAPTER 1

$\mathcal{N}$early forty-eight hours had passed since Daniel had left the prison after his brief visit with Annabelle. He was standing on the balcony of his hotel with a glass of red wine in his hand, overlooking the skyline at Mandarin Oriental. One of the exclusive places to stay in Atlanta's popular area called Buckhead. He held his phone in one hand with it on speaker, impatiently waiting to be connected to someone at the prison where Annabelle was incarcerated and, finally, after few moments, a woman answered.

"Yes, this is Daniel Thomas and I'm calling with great concerns about Annabelle Humphrey. I was just there at your facility two days ago and I was escorted out in a rush because of some sort of emergency. And since that day, I haven't heard from my client and I will not get off the phone until I can speak with her or at least find out what is going on."

The woman on the other end listened to him patiently without interruption and, then, she responded, "Mr. Thomas, I sincerely understand your concerns about her and, unfortunately, I'm unable to do either. I can put you through to the warden. Hold please," she said, and he was put on hold without agreeing to hold.

Daniel sipped on his wine and sat down at the round glass table. He placed his phone down while he waited for the warden to come on the line. He viewed the Atlanta skyline; it was beautiful, even at ten o'clock in the morning. And for six thousand dollars a night, the view itself made it all worth his wild; he thought and smiled to himself and the thoughts of Annabelle returned to his mind. The thought of Annabelle and the harsh living situation that she was in made him cringe and he wished the Warden would come on the line because the minutes that went by made him irritated. He shut his eyes and said a quick silent prayer to himself to have more patience, because the anger was brewing inside him, so he closed his eyes and took three long deep breaths.

After a few more seconds passed, a deep voice came from the other end. "Good morning Mr. Thomas, I apologize for the wait. What can I do for you this morning?" the Warden said from the other end.

"Good morning to you, sir. I'm a very good friend of Annabelle Humphrey, and I was just at your prison a couple of days ago visiting her, along with her team of attorneys and, before we could finish our business, some sort of emergency happened and she was rushed back to her dorm and our visit was terminated. As of now, I would like to know if she's alright and how soon can we visit with her again?"

"Okay, I believe I remember you and your men visiting Humphrey. It's a minor problem going on at my prison right now and that young lady is in the middle of it all," he said in a straight forward tone of voice.

"I honestly can't understand how. I'd like to know more details, so will it be at all possible for me to visit her in the morning? I flew all the way in from London just to see her and I can't go all the way back without speaking with her."

There was a long pause from the other end, then finally the warden said, "My prison is still on lockdown, which means she's still on lockdown and can't have any visitors Mr. Thomas."

Daniel smiled as he listened at the Warden's antagonistic tenor because he knew that this clown wasn't going to prevent him from seeing Annabelle and he didn't care about a lockdown. "Warden Brown, correct?" he asked.

"Yes," the Warden responded from the other end.

"Okay Warden Brown, let me tell you a little something about myself and my family."

"I don't really have the time to-" he tried to dispute.

"Oh, you will lend me your ear and your time," he responded back as a matter fact in his thick French accent.

Warden Brown must have reconsidered because he quickly replied, "You got my ear Mr. Thomas, now speak." With that, Daniel took another sip of his wine and, in a nice and calm tone of voice, he took up twenty more minutes of the Warden's time, explaining that not seeing Annabelle the next morning wasn't an option.

ANNABELLE FELT HOPELESS; she was still in her cell, lying on her bunk, with nothing to do or nowhere to go. Two days had went by and she still hadn't heard anything about her friend Black Girl, and she was going out of her mind with concern. The prison was still on lockdown and the officers weren't telling the prisoners anything, well not anything useful. She was lying on her back staring at the ceiling for maybe hours; she had lost track of time. Her cellmate worked in the kitchen and would probably be gone for several hours, so the alone time only gave her more time to think.

3

Annabelle slowly climbed down from her bunk and slipped her feet inside a pair of slides. She turned and walked towards the door and looked out the square glass window at nothing in particular. Just a spacious and empty dormitory. She took a long deep breath and, out of the blue, Daniel came to her mind. It made her smile, but she thought about how Jamal had made her smile the same exact way when she first met him too and that made her smile disappear just as fast as it came. She felt her stomach twisting in knots. Pain and bad energy washed over her and that was a feeling that she didn't want to experience ever again in her life.

But, somewhere in her spirit, she felt that Daniel was different. The Word of God had drawn him to her, nothing physical like her face, her curves, or her beauty, but the Word of God because she had no pictures on that Facebook page. While staring out the door, she thought about the way he was sitting in the chair and stood up and introduced himself to her. The Sunday school teacher, he said to her; his voice was smooth as baby skin. Annabelle smiled again and wrapped her arms around herself. She was leaning against the door.

Her mind then shifted to thoughts of Daisy Mae. "God, let her be alright," she said in a low whisper and began shaking her head side to side. Then, she heard the sally port doors open. But, from her cell, she couldn't see the front of the dorm. Several women prisoners were yelling from behind their doors.

"Hey LT, when you gonna let us off of lockdown?" she heard one inmate ask.

"It may be today," he said.

Annabelle heard footsteps running up the stairs and it sounded as if they were getting closer to her; she had her face pressed against the glass and then a round, brown, fleshy face popped up in the glass. "Humphrey," he said from the other side of the door.

Annabelle looked up at him through the glass. "Yes, that's me," she responded.

"Get dressed, the Warden wants to see you."

Annabelle stared at him for a brief moment before saying anything. "Do you know the issue?" she finally asked him.

"I'm not sure. But, I believe somebody has been calling to the prison for you, but I just can't say for sure," he said to her, and then he eased his key into the lock, turned it, and opened the door. Annabelle was already dressed in her khaki pants and shirt; while the lieutenant waited for her to put on her shoes, he was looking at her. "I hear you a very popular person in the prison," he said dryly.

Annabelle was sitting on the bottom bunk tying up her shoes; she never looked up at him when he said that. Instead, she stood when she finished; her facial expression was calm and serious. "I'm ready, sir," was all she said.

The lieutenant let out a, "Hmph," at Annabelle and then folded his arms across his massive chest. "So, apparently, you think this situation is a joke." He looked down into her eyes, giving her a cold stare.

"I don't think anything is a joke, sir," Annabelle said.

"Yeah, well, from the word around the prison, you the reason why your friend was stabbed and now she's fighting for her life."

Annabelle froze; her eyes were locked dead on his and he looked square into hers also. "I'm ready to go where I need to go," she said and walked out the cell and passed him. He came out behind her and closed the door to her cell. Annabelle stood up against the rail and allowed him to pass by, and then she followed behind him in silence. Her mind was racing at the thought of him saying that it was her fault that her friend Black Girl was stabbed.

They were moving down the stairs now. And, at that moment, one of the inmates yelled from behind one of the doors, "Hey church girl! You next!"

Annabelle pretended not to hear it as she was getting closer towards the front door; then, she heard another female voice yell out, "Annabelle, I'll deal wit' her as soon as these doors come open! We gonna show them that God got warriors too!"

Abruptly, the lieutenant stopped, and he turned around and addressed the entire dorm. "As long as I know it's a so called war going on, ain't nobody coming off of lockdown."

Annabelle couldn't do anything but shake her head in disgust at what she heard out of his mouth. They walked through the sally port doors and on outside. When he walked up the sidewalk with her, they were in silence. He began whistling an old country tune; Annabelle looked at him as they walked. "You said she was fighting for her life. I appreciate you for telling me that. Just a confirmation from God that my sister is alright."

The lieutenant silenced his whistling and looked at her; he slowed his pace down and then stopped. "I heard she's alright, hopefully that'll help," he revealed to her.

Annabelle nodded her head up and down; then, they began walking again in silence. It only took them a few minutes to get to the Warden's office. The lieutenant knocked on the door while Annabelle stood alongside of him in silence. When the voice from inside said, "Come in," the officer turned the knob and walked inside, and then held the door open for Annabelle to come in. She lifted her head and shoulders and moved inside the office. The Warden was sitting behind a mahogany desk with his fingers pressed together. "Good morning, Humphrey," he said. His eyes fixed dead on her.

"Good morning, Warden Brown," she responded.

"Have a seat," he said to her.

Annabelle sat down in the chair in front of his desk. The warden then looked up at the lieutenant that was still standing at the door, as if he was a bouncer at a club or something. "Let me have a minute with her alone, Lieutenant Green," he said.

He gave the warden a look as if needed to stay, but he followed orders and slowly nodded his head, turned on his heel, and exited the office and closed the door behind him. When it clicked shut, the Warden's eyes went to Annabelle; he sat up in his chair a little. "Now, you were just in here a couple of days ago. Had all these big fancy lawyers from Atlanta to come see you. And now this so called millionaire guy from London is calling every hour on the hour with threats of the whole entire prison if he don't speak with you. Now, before we go any further, I have a couple of questions for you."

Annabelle sat and stared at him, she crossed her legs, smiled, and said, "I'm listening."

Warden Brown's eyes never left Annabelle. And it seemed as if they were trying to see who would break first. He cleared his throat. "What is going on in my prison with you and the Bloods?"

"Warden Brown, I'm nothing more than a woman of Christ, and I'm sure you know that when God calls someone home, you can't stop it, or when he calls someone to do his work, you can't stop that either," she paused and took a deep breath. Then, she had to clear her throat as well. "I'm walking the path that I have no control over. There are several women in this prison that were gang members, several women that didn't have any direction in life. Several women that never read the Bible and even more that don't pray or even believe in God. However, and I'm sure you know this, but when you a child of God and work for him,

7

the Devil is going to work in double overtime to stop that. Right."

He nodded his head, listening intently.

Annabelle went on. "I'm not trying to cause any trouble in your prison, Warden Brown. But, the devil don't like to see people doing the work of the Lord, so he send his people that works for him to disrupt all the good," she paused again, now her eyes were turning moist; she looked down at the floor and she looked back at him. "My friend Angel that was stabbed, we lived in a women's shelter together in Atlanta and didn't know each other from a can of paint. The day we met, I was praying in the shelter; she walked up behind me and asked me to say a prayer for her because she was about to use a stolen credit card to get her son some clothes. That day we held hands and I prayed for her, we prayed together. All that was God's plan. We went our separate ways and we met again under these circumstances. I'm passionate about a lot of things, sir. And I must admit, I'm very emotional. The day that I met Angel in here in prison is the day that she saved me from Bloods; I didn't come from that type of life, so I wasn't familiar with any of it until I came here. So, when I heard that she was stabbed and on her death bed, I couldn't do anything but pray about it. I even asked him why. And you know what his response was?"

"No, what was it?" he asked.

"God said to me, I never said that the weapons wouldn't form, I only said that they wouldn't prosper."

Warden Brown's face had a look on it as if he couldn't believe what he was hearing, more like pain and sorrow all bundled together. He began shaking his head side to side, as if what she had just told him made him feel like Annabelle was his daughter sitting in front of him telling him that she was in trouble and didn't know what to do. Now, with a long stare and a moment of silence, he took a deep breath. "I... I don't even know what to say to that."

"Well, you can start off by saying that God is good," she responded.

"God is good," Warden Brown said and, then, he eased his fingers down inside his shirt around the collar as if he wanted to loosen it. Then, he finally said. "I've heard enough about that; I'm going to let you make a phone call." His hands were trembling a little bit for some unapparent reason. He pushed his chair back and stood up. He turned the phone towards Annabelle and handed her a number that was written down on a yellow sticky note. "I'm going to step outside in the hallway and give you a few minutes of privacy, okay."

Annabelle took the phone and nodded her head at him. "Thank you, sir," she said to him and slid up to the edge of her chair. She looked down at the yellow sticky note and memorized the number, just as Warden Brown was walking out of the office; the door closed behind her and she dialed the number.

CHAPTER 2

"*Y*es, Daniel speaking," his French accent came through the phone.

Annabelle's face lit up like a Christmas tree. "Hello, Daniel," she said cheerfully and happy to hear his voice.

"Annabelle, my God. Are you alright?" he asked. She could hear the excitement in his voice and that made her smile ever brighter.

Annabelle couldn't hide it any longer; she tried to contain herself. Her heart started to beat rapidly and butterflies danced in her stomach. She gripped the phone a little tighter, and then she said, "Yes, I'm fine and blessed."

"That's wonderful. Well, I see the Warden is a man of his word, even though I had to go to the extreme to get you on the phone. No worries though, God will always come through for us. So, before we go any further, will you say a quick prayer for us and everyone around us?"

Annabelle took a breath, her eyes slowly closed. "Yes, are you ready?"

"Yes, I am."

"Dear Lord, today is so special to me, to us, and everyone around us. This morning, this prayer is from me but not for me. First off, I'm asking you to heal my best friend Angel, hold her hand Father. Hold her heart and keep her covered in your precious blood. Regardless of the facts, we know that you have the final word. For sister Daisy Mae, I haven't spoken with her either, but I ask you to remove all illness and bad health away from her mind, body, and soul. I'm speaking to you Father on the behalf of everyone that needs prayer. Also Father, I ask you to continue to bless Daniel, watch over him, protect him, and continue to guide him in the right direction. In Jesus' name we pray. Amen."

"Amen," Daniel said. Then, he added, "And dear Father, I ask that you protect Annabelle as she goes through these trials and tribulations of her incarcerations. I ask you to remove her from prison, protect her from her enemies and anyone that has hatred for her. Amen."

Annabelle nodded and smiled. "Amen," she said again.

"As of now, what do you need me to do while I'm still here?" Daniel asked her.

"Are you still in Atlanta?" she asked him.

"Yes I am," he responded.

"My dear friend, sister Daisy Mae is there. I spoke with her days ago and I'm not really sure if she is in good health or if she has anyone helping her."

"Annabelle, what is it that you need me to do? You want me to bring her to see you? If so, it's not a problem."

Annabelle's heart felt as if it was melting inside of her chest; she wasn't even thinking about seeing sister Daisy, but she most certainly wanted to. "Will you bring her to see me?" she asked in the sweetest tone of voice.

"Of course I will," Daniel said; he paused briefly. "Listen, I'm not sure if you're taking me serious or not. But whatever you need me to do, I'll do it. Do you not realize that you saved my life?"

"How, Daniel?" she asked. Her voice was low and filled with an urgency that had her ready to hear what he had to say.

"In due time, I'll tell you. I'd rather it be face to face. Or even better, once you're home over dinner."

Annabelle smiled, her eyes watered, and all she could do was shake her head side to side at the thought of going home. What he was saying was soothing to her ears. Then, she said, "I'm patient, Daniel."

"Thank you, Annabelle. We know that God doesn't make mistakes. Now, give me sister Daisy address and phone number." She rattled off the information.

"And can I ask you one more favor?" she added. "Can you find out where my friend Angel Hamilton is? That day when all of the commotion took place, she was stabbed and hurt pretty bad. I don't know where she is or how she is truly doing, to be honest."

"Enough said, don't worry about anything Annabelle. I'll find out for you."

"Thank you," she said and they chatted a little longer. Annabelle was grateful that the warden allowed her time to speak with him and alone. Daniel assured her that he'd call her back soon and come see her as soon as he could. With that, she went back to her cell with a wide grin plastered on her face.

* * *

OVER TWENTY STAB wounds Black Girl had endured, and it was only one fatal one that punctured her lung and caused her to nearly lose her life. She was now laid up in the hospital bed, breathing through a ventilator tube and with another chest tube wedged through her ribs and surrounding her lungs to slowly remove the air. Inside the ICU room was a doctor, he was tall and slim with a neat beard and wearing a white jacket over his suit. There were also two correctional officers from the prison that was there with her.

One of them was inside the room with her. He was sitting in the corner in a chair with a gun magazine in his hands, like he didn't have a care in the world. In his mid-fifties Daniel assumed, the older white man couldn't care less if this convict lived or died; he was just there to collect a paycheck. When Daniel walked in and the officer realized he wasn't one of the doctors, he looked up from the magazine, tilted his head to the side a little bit, and then stood to address Daniel before he could greet the doctor. "Who are you?" he questioned. "This young lady isn't allowed any visitors," he said.

"Don't worry, the warden knows I'm here. You can check with the officer outside the door if you like."

He nodded and went back to the chair that he couldn't wait to plant his bottom back in. After his nose was back into his magazine, Daniel turned to the doctor. "How is she doing?" he asked him with true concern.

The doctor was making a few adjustments to the equipment that Angel was connected to. He paused and turned his attention to Daniel. "She's doing better and she's definitely a fighter. It normally takes six to eight weeks to fully recover from a punctured lung. This is day two, so we have a ways to go, but she will be okay."

Daniel nodded his head while staring down at her. The sight of her lying there with tubes in her nose and in her mouth brought a deep sadness over him. To have to suffer like that was a terrible sight to see. "So, how many times was she actually stabbed?" Daniel asked.

The doctor pulled the chart from the bed and scribbled a

note. "Unfortunately nineteen times, but most of them wasn't deep punctures; she blocked that with her arms I'm guessing because her injuries to her arms were the majority. But, for the most part, she'll be fine. A lot of the punctures were defensive wounds and that is a miracle if you ask me."

"Well, that's good to hear," he said, his voice lowered. Then, he added, "This girl was a gang member, but then gave her life to Christ and this was her punishment for wanting to do better. I mean, for Christ sakes," he sighed, shaking his head side to side in disgust.

The doctor looked over at him; he put his hand on his shoulder. "She's going to be alright; she's tough and we most certainly know that she's one of God's angels."

Daniel nodded his head, with his eyes on her. Then, he looked up at the doctor. "How long will it be before she's able to get up and walk? I mean, the prison has an infirmary, so I'm sure they want to get her back there as quickly as they can."

"The prison infirmary isn't capable of taking care of this kind of situation, so she'll be here for a long while before I release her." With that, Daniel touched Angel's hand and prayed before he left the room. When he was in his car, he called the Warden and gave him the information Annabelle would need to talk to her doctor.

CHAPTER 3

*B*lack Girl had her eyes closed, but she was finally waking up and she could hear voices. She was in a little discomfort, but not the same pain she had experienced the day of her attack. What she had heard the doctor say about her surviving the brutal attack made her feel relieved and she knew it was a true blessing to be alive. She was grateful that she was in in a real hospital and not at the prison. She tried to open her lids, but to no avail, so she just relaxed. She thought about Annabelle, her best friend and she wondered if word had gotten back to her about how she was doing, because she knew Annabelle would be going insane not know that she was okay.

She knew she had to be strong and fight her way back and get well as fast as her body would allow her. Her eyes formed tears and, even though she had turned her life around, they would pay for what they did to her, she thought. She immediately thought of the scriptures. *Dearly beloved, avenge not yourselves, but rather give place unto wrath: for it is written, Vengeance is mine; I will repay, saith the Lord.*

Romans 12:19. Black Girl knew that was the voice of God immediately correcting her thoughts.

Black Girl's eyes were closed; her eyes even tight. Her mind was racing at a speed of two hundred miles per hour as the word of God began to quicken her spirit. Scriptures about forgiveness, God's grace, and His promises of good things to come gave her peace, and the thoughts of making them pay slowly released from her heart and her thoughts. She realized at that moment that the spirit of God was truly inside of her and God had saved her life. She silently prayed, praised, and gave thanks to God for her life and for bringing her out of the darkness, into his holy light.

Just then, she heard the doctor's phone sound off. "Doctor Foley speaking," he said and, then, Angel guessed he put the call on speaker because she heard Annabelle's voice.

"Doctor Foley. Good morning, my name is Annabelle Humphrey and I'm calling about Angel Hamilton."

"She's doing well; it'll be a couple weeks before she's up and moving, but my patient is going to be just fine, she is going to pull through," he said.

"That's so great to hear," Annabelle said, then she added, "Only, God."

Black Girl was so happy to hear Annabelle's voice that she opened her eyes; she tried to speak, but the tube had her voice low and hoarse. "Belle," was the only word that escaped her mouth.

"Wait a minute, it looks like she's awake. You may not be able to hear her clearly, but you are on speaker if you want to speak to her. "How are you feeling?" he asked Angel.

"Belle," she repeated.

"Bell?" he said, confused. "I don't understand," he paused. "She's actually trying to talk right now, but I don't know what she's saying."

"Can she hear me?" Annabelle asked the doctor.

"Yes, I have you on speaker." He pushed the phone closer to her face.

"Angel... if you can hear me, just know that you'll be out of there soon and we all love you... I'm so sorry that this happened to you," Annabelle's word choked up and Angel could hear her crying. "I... am sorry." She was sniffling out loud.

"Belle," Black Girl whispered again. She tried to get out a sentence but felt short of breath.

"Yes, I hear you, Angel," Annabelle said; she was finding her voice again. "I have to get off the phone now; get you some rest and I'll see you soon. God is good."

All... the... time, Black Girl thought to herself. Then, she closed her eyes and a tear rolled down the side of her face.

CHAPTER 4

*I*t was nine forty-two the following morning, Daisy Mae was up, sitting at her kitchen table reading the Atlanta Journal Constitution and sipping on a hot cup of Folgers coffee. She sat the paper down, picked up the cup and took a small sip. Daisy Mae had a thing for black coffee and, every time she tasted it, she had to close her eyes to savor the flavor. When she sat the cup back down, her hand shook a little. Then, the phone rang and, by the second ring, she stood to her feet. "Lord ham mercy, Jesus," she whispered and wobbled on over to the wall where the phone was at. On the fourth ring, she picked it up. "Hello."

"Good morning, Miss Daisy Mae."

"Good morning and, whatever you trying to sell, I already bought it."

"No, I'm not a salesperson."

"Well, thank you anyway baby. And God bless you okay," she said politely and then hung up the phone. Daisy Mae moved back towards the table. She looked down at her cup of coffee; the steam was still coming off the top of it. She picked it up with both hands; she felt herself trembling again as she took a sip. And just as she was sitting the cup back down, her doorbell rang, the sounds chimed throughout the house. She turned around, pulled her housecoat closer around her body and, with her side to side wobble, she moved towards the front door. When she went to the window near the door and slightly parted the curtains, she saw the white guy standing out on her front porch. And to her, he was either a bill collector or he was trying to sell something. She snatched the door open.

"Listen, I'm not interested in whatever it is you're selling," she quickly said.

"No, Miss Daisy Mae, I'm not selling anything. Your friend Annabelle sent me here to check on you."

Daisy Mae's eyebrows bunched together. She leaned forward, so she could hear him clearer. "What you say?" she asked.

"I said Annabelle Humphrey sent me," he said again, looking down at her with a calm aura over him.

She unlocked the screen door and pushed it open. He stood there in front of her; she looked up at his face. "Is she alright?" she asked him.

"Yes ma'am, she is. My name is Daniel, Daniel Thomas." He smiled and then extended his hand out to her. When she shook it, he said, "I'm a good friend of Annabelle's and the man you just hung up on a few moments ago," he laughed.

Daisy Mae laughed lightly with him. "Baby, I'm so sorry," she said. "Now, come on in." She stepped back and allowed him to come in. He came across the threshold and stepped to the side and allowed her to close the door.

"Have a seat baby," she said and began walking towards the kitchen. "Let me get you a good hot cup of coffee," she said as she walked.

Daniel sat down on the sofa. "Thank you, that would be great," he said. Daisy Mae came back from the kitchen holding a cup of hot coffee for him. She walked up to him and handed it to him. "Thank you, ma'am," he said politely as he took the cup from her.

"You're welcome, and you don't sound like you from here talking like that. You sound like the white man from the Old Spice commercial."

Daniel was just about to sip his coffee when she said that and he nearly spilled it at the hilarious comment. He pulled the cup down from his face and had to laugh at that himself. After he took a tiny sip, he put the cup on the coffee table and looked up at her. "I'm from London."

"London! What you doing way over here?" She sat down in her chair across from him and crossed her legs at the ankles, staring straight at him.

Daniel picked up the cup, took a sip of coffee, and sat it back down. "Actually, I'm here for Annabelle. I'm a real good friend of hers and she asked me to drop in and check on you and to bring you to see her."

"Are you serious?" Daisy Mae asked.

"Yes, I told her I would bring you to visit her. She says you're like her mother to her, so I can't mess this up." He smiled.

Daisy Mae was staring at him long and hard, not really knowing what to say. Then, suddenly, it just came out. "The doctor told me I got six months to live, and I told Annabelle that I only had a lump because I didn't want to worry her while she was in there." She slightly dropped her head for a second and stared at the floor.

"And that's what the doctor said?"

She nodded her head without even looking up at him.

"Well, what did God say?"

Daisy Mae raised her head. When she looked at him, she had tears in her eyes, but then the words he said made her smile. "He has the final say so," she responded back.

Daniel was nodding his head up and down, agreeing, and then he asked her. "Have you started your treatment?"

There was another long pause from Daisy Mae; she took a deep breath. "I did, but I haven't been going like I should. I turned eighty years old last month."

"And what that does that mean?" He asked. "A lot of people would love to see eighty years old, I know I do. And I want to be around to see you turn one hundred."

"I want to see that as well," she said softly. She knew she sounded like she had given up already and didn't have any enthusiasm what so ever. "I can't let Annabelle know my situation; her mother died from cancer and, if she finds out the truth, she will fall apart in that prison."

Daniel sat in silence for a minute or two. He just looked at Daisy Mae, and the look on his face was clear that things were dancing around in his mind about her. He then pulled out his iPhone and dialed a number and put his phone on speaker; it rang three times before someone answered. "Good morning," the voice said.

"Good morning, Paul."

"How's it going in the United States?"

"It is wonderful; God brought me in the presence of some beautiful blessed people."

"That's great, sir. Are you coming home anytime soon?"

"I believe so," he said, and then he looked at Daisy Mae. "Would you like to go to London with me?"

Daisy Mae shook her head. "Oh no, baby," her voice was low. "I don't fly on nobody airplanes," she chuckled, but she was dead serious.

He laughed a little. "Do me a favor, Paul. Will you please locate the best cancer doctor in the world, the U.S., or even better in Atlanta, or somewhere close that won't be too long of a drive?"

"Oh my God, Daniel. Do you have cancer?"

Daniel hesitated for a minute; he was staring at Daisy Mae. "No, but a lady that's like a mother to Annabelle does. So, please find the best for us because Daisy Mae has made it perfectly clear that she will not get on anyone's aircraft."

"Yes sir, I will and, as soon as were done, I'm on it," he said and hung up.

Daisy Mae's eyes were fixed dead on Daniel's and her heart warmed. She desperately tried to hold her tears back, but she couldn't. She stood up and walked over to him, and he stood up himself because he knew what she was coming for. Then, she wrapped her arms around him. "Thank you. But, please don't tell Annabelle."

"I won't," he whispered.

"I don't know why you'd be interested in doing something so great for me, but I'm grateful."

"When God puts someone in a position to help another, that is exactly what we are supposed to do. I'd do the same for a stranger on the street, so it's my pleasure to help you, Daisy Mae, and Annabelle is special to me and anything I can do to help her and the people she loves, consider it done."

Daisy Mae nodded her head up and down, even though she felt like that she was too old to be going through surgery and treatments. However, at this point, she recognized that it was bigger than her. "Okay," her voice was a mere whisper.

* * *

"Now, what I want to do, I only heard bits and pieces about Annabelle and the situation that got her in prison," he sat down. Then, he said to Daisy Mae. "Sit for a minute, please."

She took a few steps backwards and found the seat that she was just sitting in. When she sat down, he asked, "Why did the members of the church that Annabelle attended turn their back on her?"

"Oh baby, that story can go forever," she said and took a deep breath and started shaking her head side to side. She went on. "Mt. Calvary church is small. And the members can be wishy washy, if you know what I mean. Pastor James is a pretty decent man, I would say. But, just like any church in America, everybody has flaws and everybody sins, and that's including the pastors, deacons, and Bishops. Now, the problems come when the members of any congregation looks at the head of the church as if they are Jesus himself."

"Hmmm," Daniel let out.

"Right. And the situation with Annabelle and the Pastor's brother sent the church into an uproar, and I wasn't about to turn my back on Annabelle because her sin wasn't any different than stealing from Walmart. But, everyone has their own overly righteous opinions. I look at her like she's my own child and, when I decided to support her, the church didn't like my decision."

Daniel folded his arms across his chest; his eyes went to the floor and then back up to her. There were so many things that he wanted to say and ask, but he knew that it would take longer than he planned to stay. So, after a few minutes of silence between the both of them, he said, "What do you think about me going to meet with Pastor James one day?"

Daisy Mae shrugged her shoulders. "I don't know, but what I do know is that I'm no longer a member there." Her shoulders shrugged as well and then her hands opened and shut.

Daniel nodded. "Just a thought I guess." He took a deep breath, then stood to his feet and held both of his hands out to her. "Will you pray with me?" he asked her.

Daisy Mae gave a look as if to be saying, *you should know I will.* She slowly stood to her feet and let out a small grunt. Then, she walked to him and placed her hands inside of his. Daniel squeezed her hands and bowed his head.

"Dear Father," he said, lowering his voice. "My prayers to you this morning is to allow me every chance and opportunity to help strengthen Miss Daisy Mae and her back to good health. I ask you to combine our prayers, combine our positive energy, and remove any and all negative energy away from our lives. Today, I have learned a few things, one of them is that Miss Daisy Mae is the most kindhearted and good spirited women that I've met in a long time and, even though I totally disagree with any illness that the doctors says she has, I'm also asking you Father, please remove it and cover her with your blood. Amen."

"Amen!" she whispered. "And thank you, Daniel." She opened her eyes and looked at him. "Are you gon' get my baby out of that prison?"

He smiled. "Yes, God has confirmed it. So, yes," he said in a reassuring tone of voice.

"Well, with that being said, I need to be alive and well when she comes home. And wherever I need to fly to, I'm ready," she smirked with a nod.

"That is a good decision because it's worth your health," he said and then pulled her into a tight hug.

CHAPTER 5

*D*ays passed and finally lockdown was over and, although she was in prison, she felt free. All of the doors were opened at the same time and everyone started spilling out into the dayroom area; several of the women were cheering with joy and some of them were racing towards the showers. Annabelle was still in her cell sitting at the desk, taking notes from her Bible. Then, her door came open. Annabelle looked up at an angry inmate coming through the door. She stood at six foot two with long arms, high cheekbones, and broad shoulders. She stopped just inside the door and closed it behind her. She pulled up her shirt, and there were four prison-made knives lined around her waist with handles made from torn sheets and braided perfectly. Annabelle stood up; the tall girl pulled one of them out of her waist. The blade was long and flat with a sharp point. When she extended it out towards Annabelle, she was holding it by the blade. Annabelle held out her hand and the handle fell into it. "Do you really believe that I will need this?" she asked.

"Once again, Annabelle. We just seen our sister nearly get killed up in here." She pointed towards the floor. "They're sending threats that you are next. And I'm not going to let that happen. The same way the Muslims ride for each other, the Christians are about to ride the same way." The huge woman growled.

Annabelle took a deep breath; then, she stuffed the knife in her waist, and then three more women were standing at the door. They walked in one by one behind each other. The first girl was short and stocky and she walked like she meant business. She gave Annabelle a hug. "Good to see you," she said to her.

"Good to see you too, Tasha," Annabelle returned. Tasha turned and looked up at the first girl that walked in with the weapons.

"How you doing, Charlene?" she asked her.

Charlene leaned down and hugged her. "Hey, Tasha," she said. Then, she looked at the other two girls. "Hey, Angie. Hey, Precious."

Everybody spoke to each other and, then, they all chatted for the next few minutes, discussing the issue about Black Girl and the female Blood members. Charlene gave out a knife to everyone in the room and they all formed a circle and held hands and, just as they were about to start praying, someone alerted the dorm that the police was coming in downstairs. Charlene was the first one that went to the door and peeped out. "Three cert team officers just entered," she said as she turned around. "They look like they moving fast and looking for somebody." She raised her shirt and held out her hands. "Everybody give me the knives," she demanded anxiously.

One by one, she received the knives and eased them back into her waist and smoothed her shirt back down.

"Lock it down!" one of the officers yelled. "Everybody back to your cells!"

Slow and carefully, Charlene walked out first. Annabelle went to the door and looked out before the other three girls could walk out. She saw the cert officers moving around downstairs, then a few more blue suit officers were coming in. "Ya'll come on out," she turned and whispered to them. All three of them moved towards the door and eased out one at a time and went back to their cells.

Annabelle pulled her door closed and stood there at the door for a few minutes, just to see what the officers were doing. From what she could hear was that they were at someone's room downstairs, but she couldn't actually see anything. For some apparent reason, her heart rate sped up; she knew they were coming for her. The Facebook page had been blown; then again, it may have been something about the counselor, or even worse.

"Calm down, Annabelle," she heard a voice say.

She turned and looked around as if someone was in the room with her. Finally realizing that it was God giving her confirmation again, she took a deep breath and then another one. When she looked out the glass through her door, she noticed that everyone was locked down now and it was quiet. Then, out of nowhere, she heard a female voice scream out in a rage, "So, ya'll playin' the police game now?"

Annabelle was straining her neck now to see who the lady that was screaming from downstairs. And sure enough, it was one of the members from the Blood gang, and Annabelle was sure that she was the same one that was talking from behind the door sending threats at her. When they finally packed up all of her property, they escorted her out of the dorm and, moments later, all of the doors came open again. Annabelle stepped out onto the top range and leaned up against the rail overlooking the dorm. As the women spilled out into the dorm, she said loud and clear to everyone, "God never said that the weapons wouldn't form, he only said that they wouldn't prosper." She then turned around and walked back inside of her cell, closed the door, and covered the window with a cutout piece of cardboard. After that, she got on her knees in the middle of the floor, interlocked her fingers, and said a prayer. "God, I just can't thank you enough."

Then, she heard his voice. "Through good times and bad times, I'm with you, Annabelle."

"Thank you, Father and, honestly, sometimes I have my doubts and I'm just being truthful. I'm sure I'm telling you something that you already know."

"All you need is a little faith. I'll do and show you the rest. But, faith is the path. Believe in me, believe in yourself."

"Yes, I will," she said. "Amen!"

* * *

AFTER A FEW MORE DAYS PASSED, Saturday had arrived and it was nine o'clock on the head when Annabelle's name was called across the intercom to get ready for visitation. She was already awake, sitting at her desk taking notes from her Bible. Annabelle was fully dressed and dolled up, eyeliner and lipstick. Not too much but enough to enhance her beautiful face. She stood, trying hard not to show her nervousness. But, it was next to impossible to hide. She closed her Bible, walked over towards the door, and looked at herself in the mirror; she adjusted her shirt and then her collar. *You look fine*, she said to herself.

When she arrived at the visitation room, there was a female office sitting to her left at a desk. Annabelle turned and faced her.

"Name?" she asked Annabelle.

"Annabelle Humphrey," she said and handed the lady her prison ID. Without another word, she turned around and faced the huge room that was half filled with families conversing, and it didn't take Annabelle long to spot Daniel and Daisy Mae. They were in the far left corner near the vending machines. He was waving at her, and a bright smile formed on her face. She hurried towards them, and he got up to meet her halfway. He quickly pulled her into his arms in a tight hug, and Annabelle closed her eyes and just relaxed in his arms for a long moment.

"It's so good to see you, Annabelle," he whispered in the crook of her neck.

"I had no idea you'd be here today, and you brought Daisy Mae. I'm so surprised and I'm happy to see you also, Daniel," she said cheerfully.

He pulled away from her, and a slow moving Daisy Mae just stood and waited for Annabelle to make it over to their table. "Hey baby, how have you been?" she said with her arms open to receive a hug. Annabelle walked into her embrace and they squeezed each other tighter than Annabelle ever remembered hugging a person.

"I'm good Daisy Mae and so much better now to see you. I've missed you, so much," Annabelle said and didn't want to let go. When they finally broke their hug, Annabelle's eyes teared up. She was happy and sad at the same time. Happy to have finally get a visit from them, but sad that they had to visit her behind bars. "I'm so sorry," was all she could say.

"You ain't got nothin' to be sorry for, baby," Daisy Mae said and patted Annabelle's hand. Annabelle wiped the tears, and Daisy Mae gently touched her cheek. Daniel walked up with a hand full of napkins, and he handed them each to Annabelle and they sat.

Annabelle examined Daisy Mae and then said, "Look at you, young lady, you haven't aged one bit," she teased.

"Well, I may not look it, but my old body can feel it," she said and pointed at Daniel. "You gonna marry this man here one day, I can feel it."

Annabelle flashed an embarrassing smile. "Now, where did that come from?" She brought her hand up to her lips.

Daisy Mae looked at Annabelle. "Baby, you know just as well as I know, only God himself could pull this off. Y'all was made for each other."

Annabelle looked over at Daniel, and his eyes were locked on her. "So, you agree with what she says?" she asked.

"I don't disagree," he smirked. "All I know is there is something about you that warms my heart and spirit. God only knows what our purpose for each other is and I'll wait on him to lead me," he said with a slight shoulder shrug.

Annabelle nodded, trying to hide her blush. "I agree. I mean you warm my heart and spirit too, and I constantly pray for guidance and the order of my steps. If I had listened to the Holy Spirit back then, I would have made better choices," she said, sounding as if her voice was trailing off a little.

"It's okay Annabelle. Don't beat yourself up about the choices you've made. The only thing that matters is the choices you make going forward. It's not how you start, it's how you finish. And even more, if it wasn't for this situation, we wouldn't be here right now."

"Yes ma'am, you are absolutely right," she smiled.

They were quiet for a few moments and then Daniel said, "Would you like something from the vending machine?"

She shrugged her shoulders. "Just a bottle of water, I'm not really hungry."

He stood up and looked at Daisy Mae. "What about you, Daisy Mae?"

"Bring me a Pepsi," she said in a flat tone.

Daniel shook his head. "No sodas, I'll get you a water."

She shook her head. "I might as well be laying up in Grady Memorial, he worse than the doctors."

Everyone laughed; Daniel turned and walked away, moving over towards the vending machine. After he walked away and out of distance, Annabelle said. "Why did you say that in front of him?"

"All of this is God's plan, baby," she said. "I'm not God and I don't know the final word on this, but I have good vibes about that man and I see his eyes dance when he speaks of you and I'm no fool. I see the exchanges you two make."

"He's just a good friend and he's helping me to try and get out of here."

"I know but, once that's all said and done, I don't think that will be the end of it," she said.

"I don't know, we have to wait on the Lord," Annabelle said and then asked, "What have the doctors said about the lump?"

"Oh, everything is fine on that baby, no need to worry about me." She waved her hand dismissively, as if it was nothing more to discuss about that.

"Well, that's excellent news because I was worried like crazy," Annabelle responded with relief. She had been praying day in and day out for Daisy Mae to be fine, but the look in Daisy Mae's eyes wasn't sincere, Annabelle thought, and she looked deeper at her expression.

"Why you looking at me like that?" Daisy Mae asked.

"It just seems like something else is bothering you," she said softly, her eyes dancing from one side to another as she stared into Daisy Mae's eyes.

"There is, you being in this prison is bothering me every day. I pray that you come on home, I'm gonna cook you up a feast," she said with a smile, but her eyes were glossed over and she looked down towards the floor.

Annabelle reached over and lifted up her head. "No more tears. You said the lump was not an issue and I'm okay Daisy Mae, I promise you," she said.

"I'm trying baby..." her voice trailed off. "It's so hard for me when you are sitting in prison serving a life sentence over a snake like Jamal," she expressed and then took a deep breath.

Daniel came back to the table and they both peered up at him at the same time. He was carrying their drinks and he brought a couple of bags of chips and sat everything down on the small round wooden table. When he took his seat, he looked at Annabelle and said, "I'm taking Miss Daisy Mae to London for a couple of weeks for a vacation, a much needed getaway I may add."

Annabelle's face lit up with joy. "Are you serious?" Her eyes darted from Daisy Mae to Daniel; she didn't know what to say. Then, without warning, her eyes paused on Daniel, staring at him long and hard. "God, this is a moment when I wish I wasn't in here because I'd love to go."

Daniel reached over and grabbed her hand and held it softly. "Annabelle, all you need to do is to keep praying. I'll handle everything else and soon you will be home free." Then, he kissed the back of her hand.

"I told you," Daisy Mae said. Then, she patted Annabelle on her shoulder. "He gonna be yo' husband."

Annabelle smiled and shook her head at Daisy Mae. "I guess you're going to try speaking it into existence."

"Let's get her home first, Miss Daisy Mae, and then see where things go," he said with his eyes locked on Annabelle, and the look that he was giving her had chills running up and down her spine. Annabelle didn't avert her eyes from him. She knew there was a connection, attraction, and she knew she was falling for him. She shifted her eyes from his and asked, "When are you coming back?"

"Two weeks at the latest."

For the rest of their visit, they laughed, talked, and got caught up on so many things. They talked about Angel and dreams of them both someday getting out and living the best life that they could.

CHAPTER 6

*A*s the days continued to pass, Black Girl was progressing with her health; she was now out of ICU and in a regular hospital room. It was Tuesday morning, and she was walking around an indoor track with her physical therapist, moving at a moderate pace and not too fast because of her stitches, and they hadn't completely healed. On the good side, she was clearly regaining her strength. Last week, she went through bed mobility and transfers and, by the grace of God, she was in the last stages which was called ambulation. But, Black Girl was strong in many different areas. She was mentally strong because she refused to allow this situation to keep her down, even though being stabbed could have a shellshock impact on anybody. She slowed down her pace and went over to the edge of the track and grabbed the railing; a female was walking next to her and was watching her every step. "How do you feel?" she asked Black Girl.

"Great, I just feel a tightness in the lower part of my stomach," she said and touched herself there, indicating where the pain was actually at.

The physical therapist carefully pulled her over towards a cushion bench and allowed her take a seat. "I want you to take three deep breaths real slow."

Black Girl took the first deep breath, then the second, and the third one without a problem.

"Good," the lady said. Then, she touched Black Girl's lower stomach, just around the area of her navel. With just a small press, she asked, "Any pain there?"

She shook her head and said, "No."

"Stand up for me," she said.

Black Girl stood without a problem, and a smile appeared on her face; she looked at the lady. "I don't feel anything now, like the little tingle just disappeared."

"Great, let's take it in for today," she said and got next to Black Girl, and they headed back inside the hospital. When Black Girl got back to her room, she didn't want to lie down, so she sat down in the chair and grabbed the remote to the TV and turned it on. She was tired but not exhausted. However, the best part was that she was feeling far better than she was last week. Black Girl flipped through the channels, but she didn't see anything worth watching. She stood up, walked to the window, and looked out for a minute. Black Girl stared out, lost in thought; she went back to the day that she was ambushed.

Black Girl was alone in her cell, sitting at the desk in the corner with a book called Talking With God by Adam Weber. She was just doing a little studying on how to pray better and connecting more with God. She was on chapter five in the book and the quote that she was reading came from Mother Teresa and it said, "The more you pray, the easier it becomes. The easier it becomes, the more you pray." She read that quote over and over for the next few minutes; then, she stood up and turned around and faced the bunk and got on her knees, just at the edge of the bottom bunk. Her back was to the door, so she couldn't see the girl standing behind her peeking through the rectangle shaped window in the door. Black Girl had her hands folded in front of her and her head was bowed and eyes closed.

As she said her silent prayer, she felt the draft from the door when it opened. However, that wasn't enough to stop her from praying. Five Star eased inside the room; the shank was gripped tight in her right hand and she had an angry look across her face. Suddenly, something told Black Girl to turn around and, when she did, Five Star was standing over her with the shank pulled back and she punched it through her chest. Black Girl yelled out in anger. She tried to grab Five Star, but the next stab came too fast for her; she then tried to block her face. "You gonna die today, chick," Five Star growled.

Black Girl was pouring blood now and her heart was racing uncontrollably, but she managed to roll over on her back and kicked at her. Five Star was aggressive and she wasn't trying to let up; she actually fell to the ground with Black Girl and continued to stab her and, now, she was yelling to the top of her lungs. Please God, don't let me die in here, were her thoughts; then, moments later, she passed out.

When she came out of her deep thoughts, the correctional officer from the prison had entered the room. It was the same older white guy that had been there the whole time with her, while she had been going through her healing process. "How are doing?" he asked her.

She turned around and looked at him; she allowed a small smile to appear across her face. "Hello, and yes I'm fine," she said to him. "How are you?"

"Well, I can't complain," he said while looking at her. He put his hand out in front of her. Black Girl's eyes went down to his hand; she knew as an inmate that she wasn't supposed to be shaking hands with an officer. But, she shook his hand. "I'm glad to see you doing better, you got a lot of people praying for you and cheering for you," he said and, from the sound of his voice, he did sound happy for her.

"Thanks, it's always a pleasure to hear positive news."

"Well, if you think that's some good news," he said and reached in his back pocket and pulled out a letter that was inside a folded envelope; he handed it to her.

Black Girl's heart began racing; she looked at the envelope and saw the Pardons and Parole circle logo in the top corner. She tore the envelope open and removed the letter, and she began reading. She read the entire page in silence and, when she got to the end of the letter, the bold type went: WITHIN 24 HOURS OF MY RELEASE I WILL REPORT TO MY COMMUNITY SUPERVISION OFFICER, EITHER BY PERSONAL VISIT OR BY TELEPHONE.

"Sign your name on the line young lady, you going home next week," the officer said to her with joy. Then, he handed her an ink pen. Black Girl never looked up at him; her eyes were still down on the parole papers. They were filled with tears and the drops fell onto the paper. When she finally looked up at the correctional officer, tears were just flooding her eyes and pouring down her face and, without warning, she hugged him. "This is so unreal, God is amazing," she said to him.

The officer comforted her with a warm embrace and patted her on her back. "Yes, he is," was all he said back to her.

Black Girl pulled back from him and looked at the papers again, scanning over every word to make sure that it was indeed real. After she signed the papers and gave them back to him, he said, "I don't know how the warden is going to do it; maybe you'll leave from here I would think."

"No, I need to go back to the prison first. I can't leave without seeing my sisters," she responded with a hint of urgency.

He gave a confused look; then, he shook his head side to side. "You really want to go back to the prison? It's nothing or nobody there for you," he said with a questioning look over his face.

"Oh no, you are very wrong; the prison system is not for me, but I have friends that's like real blood family members that's still there, you just don't understand."

"Maybe I don't," he responded and shrugged his shoulders all at the same time.

Black Girl finally took a deep breath; then, she wiped her eyes with her hands and looked him square in his eyes. "Mr. Officer, I grew up in the streets of Atlanta, in one of the worse neighborhoods filled with heroin, crack, and murder. Gang bangin' was only a way of life. I didn't choose that life, I didn't want to be poor, and I didn't want to come to prison. However, God had a plan for me and my life. He sat me down and gave me a better mindset and allowed me to display my talents," she paused and took a deep breath and went on. "I have a five year old son out there that's living with my mama in that same messed up neighborhood," she wiped her face again. "I don't want him to grow up like I did. I don't want him to experience this prison life and, if it wasn't for my friend Annabelle, I wouldn't even be in this state of mind. And with that being said," she paused.

The officer stood silently for a second and allowed all of her words to soak in; then, he finally said. "Hey, it's not up to me."

The following Tuesday came around fast; it was early in the morning when Black Girl returned to Lee Arrendale state prison. She was in the front passenger seat of a sixteen passenger transport van. That morning, the shift had rotated and it was a different officer that was driving her. This was actually a female correctional officer that was fairly new and hadn't been out of her black and whites but a month at the most. She looked over at Black Girl. "I know you must feel good going home today," she said.

Black Girl was staring out the window; her mind was all over the place. One minute she was thinking about Annabelle and her situation. The next minute, she was thinking about her son and how bad she wanted to change his situation. She finally looked over to her right and noticed the lady was still looking at her and waiting for a response. "Yes, it feels good," she said, but there wasn't any good energy behind her words.

The officer was backing the van in a parking space in the front of the prison. Black Girl wasn't shackled nor hand-cuffed because she was no longer an inmate. When the van had finally came to a stop, she looked around, removed her seatbelt, and opened the door. When she stepped down from the van, it seemed as if she felt an instant relief; her and the officer met up at the front of the van and they headed inside through the front of the prison.

When they got inside, Black Girl was greeted by the head warden in the front hallway. On that particular morning, he was dressed in khaki pants and a dark green collared shirt that was neatly tucked in his waist. He extended his hand out to her. "Well, Miss Hamilton," he said with a stern smile. His eyes looked her up and down. "You looking wonderful and, on top of that, you're paroling out this morning." His head was moving up and down, as if he was impressed.

Black Girl was still holding his hand, but now she had a wide grin all across her face. "Yes, God is good is all that I can say."

"Do me a favor," he said.

"Okay," she responded.

"Get out and do the right thing, there is nothing here for

you. From my understanding, you a have a son out there that needs his mother. Go raise him."

"That's the plan," she said. "I also need a favor from you, sir."

"I'm listening."

"I really need to see Annabelle Humphrey before I leave."

"No ma'am," he said while shaking his head.

"Listen, I will be on parole once I'm out and you and I both know that I will not be able to see her once I'm out. Just five minutes." She was nearly begging.

Warden Brown stared at Black Girl for a long second. "Five minutes and that's it." He then looked at the female officer that was standing right next to him. He said to her, "Tell them to send Annabelle Humphrey up here and let them know she has three minutes to get up here."

"Yes sir," she said and unclipped her walkie talkie from her side and radioed in for them to send her up.

When Annabelle walked through the front office door, she didn't have a clue as to what was going on. When Black Girl saw her, she had so many feelings turning inside of her body. She ran to Annabelle and Annabelle rushed to her as well and, when they closed their distance, they embraced right there in the corridor. "Oh my God," was the first thing that came from Annabelle's mouth as she cried and hugged her at the same time. They were cheek to cheek and they both were crying as they held each other tight. That moment seemed to go on for an hour, and Black Girl slowly pulled away from her and looked at Annabelle in her eyes. "I made parole, I'm going home this morning," she whispered.

Annabelle stood in shock; she was frozen like a deer in a set of headlights. "Are you serious?"

Black Girl nodded. "Yes, very serious. And I wasn't leaving until I seen you."

The biggest smile ever appeared across her face. "Look at God." Tears streamed down face, and she hugged Black Girl again and they both cried together again.

"I wish I could take you with me, honest to God," Black Girl said in between tears.

"I wish I could go with you," Annabelle said and hugged her even tighter. When she pulled back, she said. "All I ask of you, Angel, is to do the right thing and stay on your path. And keep in touch with me."

"Well, if that's all you asking, you not asking for enough," she said and, then, she reached for Annabelle's hands and, when their hands clasped together, Black Girl began to pray. "Dear Father, the first time you brought Annabelle and me together, it was a bond that you created. We were both at our lowest points in life, thank you for connecting us. Thank you for bringing this young lady into my life and allowing her to help me know you. I know you now, and I don't want to not know you again. I pray and ask you to protect her while she's here in this prison. Keep her safe and covered and bring her home, so we can conquer the world together. In Jesus' name we pray. Amen."

"Amen and Father, keep your hands and eyes on Angel as she enters back into the free world; we all know that it can be tough out there and even more tempting. One day we will reunite under better circumstances. I'm claiming that and standing firm on it. Thank you again Father."

Then, Annabelle leaned in and whispered in her ear, "Remember this. The Sunday school teacher is the login. The password is God is good. Everything lowercase."

Black Girl nodded her head. They hugged once again. "I love you."

"I love you, too," Annabelle said. Then, she turned and walked away without saying another word to her. Tears began pushing up again in Annabelle's eyes and her heart was hurting from pain and joy.

Black Girl stood there and watched her walk down the aisle; her eyes were swollen from the tears. She placed her hands over her chest and tilted her head sideways as she watched her disappear through the door.

BOOK 2

LONDON, ENGLAND

CHAPTER 7

*D*aniel's estate was contemporary and modern with three stories, all white, and glass and in a secluded area with automatic sliding gates. He was standing in the front of his estate looking down the driveway as the gates rolled open. Looking at the Mercedes Benz Maybach creep up the winding driveway towards him. When the Maybach pulled in front of him and came to a stop, the driver stepped out and looked at Daniel with a smile. "Good morning, sir," he said. He walked around to the passenger side rear door of the Maybach and opened it; a handsome and well-groomed man stepped out. He was in a three-piece gray suit and expensive shoes. Daniel walked up to him and met him with a smile and his hand out. "Doctor, Delehanty," he said. "Good morning, sir."

Doctor Delehanty was a tall lean man with a golden tan and black sleek hair, he stood over Daniel and grab his hand with a firm grip. "Good morning," he responded back in French.

"Come with me," Daniel said. He turned and headed towards the glass front door and the doctor followed closely behind him. There was a lady standing there in the foyer as they entered; she wore a dress and a clean apron over the outside of it. She greeted everyone with a smile and a nod. Daniel said something to her in French, and she hurried upstairs and came back down with Daisy Mae. Doctor Delehanty and Daniel was standing there in the middle of the floor watching the elderly woman being escorted down the stairs. When she made it to the bottom of the stairs, she eyed the stranger that stood near Daniel. She smiled and went and stood next to Daniel. "Good morning," she said.

Daniel said good morning and then he introduced her to the doctor. They exchanged their good mornings and then the three of them sat down in the living room on the white sofas around a huge white glass coffee table. The maid brought tea for the three of them and they all talked for the next hour; the doctor shared a lot of valuable information concerning stage four cancer. The main thing that he told her about was stem cell treatment that could be pretty pricy, but Daniel had told him that the price and money wasn't an issue. Then, he went on talking the Car-T cell therapy.

"Car-T cell therapy, what is that?" Daniel asked; he was in tune and concerned about the process just as well.

DOCTOR DELEHANTY TOOK A DEEP BREATH; then, he crossed his legs and seemed to be looking at the both of them at the same time. "Car-T cell has been a proven method for cancer patients, but also there are several side effects that has been causing problems for the nervous systems; in some people, it has caused stomach tears and also hepatitis B infection. And, then, in some women, it hasn't been any side effects at all."

Everyone sat in silence for a moment and, then, Daisy Mae said, "I just want to live long enough to see my baby come home."

Daniel reached over and grabbed her hand and held it into both of his; then, he patted it on the back. "You will see her come home," he said to her. Then, he looked back at the doctor. "We want the best treatment that money can buy. And we want to get started as soon as possible."

"Understood," was all the doctor said. His eyes reassured that he could back up his words.

* * *

THE FOLLOWING DAY, Daisy Mae was admitted into London Bridge hospital's private care, where her process started immediately. Daniel had also hired four nurses to sit with her during the process, to ensure that she was well taken care of from the hospital and back to the estate. If surgery would happen today or within the next few days, that would be perfect for Daniel. Before he left the hospital, he went inside one of the private waiting rooms and found a seat in the corner. He opened his laptop on his lap and punched in his password and went into his word document and began typing.

Hello Annabelle,

By the time this letter reaches you, I pray that it finds you in great health and good spirits. As of now, we are in London and I have Miss Daisy Mae at one of the best hospitals here. Allow me to share something with you. Miss Daisy Mae is a little sick, but she didn't want you to know because she didn't want you to worry yourself while you were inside that prison. I gave her my word that I would keep it a secret. However, on the flip side, I can't tell a lie to the woman that I'm in love with. I really didn't want to say this face to face because I couldn't find the correct words to say it to you then. And it's funny that now we're so many miles away from each other and I can say it at ease. And I'm sure that God set this up like this, at least I hope that he did anyway. I do have a few plans for us once you are out of there. One is that I pray that you will marry me one day. It's nothing to rush about once you're home. Secondly, I don't have any kids because I've been working all my life under my father and his empire. I haven't had any time to live my own life. He actually took my life and tried to make me be what he wanted me to be. He tried to set me up with the women that he wanted me to marry. I got tired of living my life through him and went out on my own. I turned to drugs and alcohol, and then I cost him and my family to lose over two hundred million dollars. After that I became the outcast of the family, I was later admitted into a private rehab here in London. But, it didn't work for me like I thought and I went on for the next few months doing the same thing. My father refused to let me work for the family company any longer, so I decided to do my own thing. I created an app that sold for a few millions of dollars, plus a percentage of the company. Then, I purchased a high-rise building here in London. That was a great investment and it brought in lots of money, but I still felt empty inside. I still wasn't getting what I needed. So, after a few more months, I went back into the rehab in hopes of getting myself together. Drinking alcohol every day and popping pills wasn't the life that God had planned for me. The depression was taking full control of my everyday life.

I remember one day sitting in my luxurious room at the rehab; I had my computer open doing some work, crunching numbers. Then, something told me to go to Facebook, and the first thing I saw was your page: The Sunday School Teacher. I'll never forget the post that caught my eye. It was like you pulled me straight to God and you were talking straight to me. I wanted better for myself. See, sometimes, it doesn't matter how much money a person has; if you don't have God in your life and there is no happiness in your home, it just will not work. At least for me anyway. I have never been married before, nor do I have any children. I want both, and I want it to be with you. My challenge was I didn't realize that you were in prison. And after I found out that made the challenge even better because I knew that God brought you to me for a reason. But, the funny part is when you blocked me. We'll tell our kids and grandkids that story for many years to come. However, it's not all about me, Annabelle. I want you to tell me what you want out of life. I also would like to know if I am the type of man that you want to spend the rest of your life with. Now, I know I'm not perfect; I snore and my feet stink after I work out. Just wanted to make you laugh a little. I'm about to end this letter now. Trust me, you don't have anything to worry about. I love you, Annabelle, and please be sure to write me back at your earliest convenience. I've never been more happier in my whole entire life since I've met you.

I want you to be free from anxieties. The unmarried man is anxious about the things of the Lord, how to please the Lord. But, the married man is anxious about the worldly things, how to please his wife, and his interests are divided. And the unmarried or betrothed women is anxious about the things of the Lord, how to be holy in body and in spirit. But, the married woman is anxious about worldly things, how to please her husband. I say this for your own benefit, not to lay any restraints upon you, but to promote good order and to secure your undivided devotion to the Lord.

1 Corinthians 7:32-35

* * *

ANNABELLE RECEIVED the letter from Daniel three days later; she was sitting in her room reading it. At first, she was looking worried about what he was saying about Daisy Mae;

that part wasn't sitting well with her at all, but the part about him saying that he couldn't tell a lie to the woman that he was in love with made her eyes tear up. Annabelle took a deep breath at that part and kept reading. Her eyes moving from one side of the letter to the other side; she smiled as she went. The letter had her heart jumping and made butterflies inside her stomach. She stood up; then, she climbed up in her bunk and continued to read the letter. She was lying flat on her back; this was her second time reading the letter to make sure that she was understood correctly.

"Are you sure you want to marry me, Daniel?" she said aloud, talking to herself, but she was bursting on the inside. Then, she brought the letter to her breasts and hugged it as if it was him that she holding in her arms. Annabelle was lost in her thoughts. She knew God had something bigger and better for her, but she didn't see this coming. Tears were slowly flowing down her cheeks, but these were the tears that she didn't want to go away. Tears of joy weren't meant to be wiped away; you just wanted to let them flow, didn't care if they soaked your shirt or not. She finally sat up in her bunk; then, she turned over on her stomach and placed her hands together and closed her eyes and said a prayer in silence. Her mind was racing as she prayed, but she was feeling wonderful on the inside.

"Amen," she said. Then, she got back up; her feelings and emotions were all over the place. She climbed out of the bunk and sat down at her desk with her pen in hand. She thought for a second and then began writing.

Dear Daniel,

I have read your letter a few times, and I've cried every time. While your words were very unexpected, they filled my heart and soul with so much happiness. You see, I have had a tough life. I grew up poor with no father and my mother was on drugs. As a child, I longed for love and affection that I just never seemed to receive. I prayed that God would send someone into my life to love me. I thought if I gave love that it would come back to me. So, even though my Mom was on drugs and neglected me, I still loved her. Then, she got clean and turned her life over to God, and he took her from. Honestly, I haven't been right ever since then. But, my prayers and faith kept me going. Even though I never knew my father, I still loved him as well. Even though we didn't have much food in our house and the water and power was off more often than on, I still gave love to everyone I met. I moved from house to house, from family member to family member, just hoping that someone would care about me. Eventually, I ended up in Atlanta at a women's shelter and found a church home that I loved. I love children because they are so innocent and give love freely. That's why I became the Sunday School Teacher. I was so happy in the church. I thought I'd finally found the place where I could receive love. Then, I met a man in the church and fell in love. Everything seemed so perfect. Just like my life was a fairy-tale. But, then, it seemed as though love failed me. How can I give so much love and not get it back? How can I try to do everything right and it goes so wrong? All I ever wanted was someone to love me. How is that so wrong? I want to love, be in love, and have someone love me back. But, I am not sure if that exists in this world.

I am glad my Facebook posts blessed you. I was actually ministering to myself, but I guess the message was needed by others also. I would love to learn more about you and your life. I guess you never know what God has in store for you. You never know why you go through different trials and tribulations. I am learning that we go through things to strengthen us mentally and spiritually. We go through stages in life to prepare us for the next stage. It has been tough in here, but God has allowed me to bless so many people. I just try to spread love. I guess, hoping to someday get the same love back that I give. I believe that's what everyone wants…. to be loved. As I read your letter, I realize that you said all of the words I wanted to hear. Those beautiful words I have longed for from a man my entire life, and yet I am so afraid to receive them. I am so afraid to be hurt again. I am afraid to believe that someone would really love me the way you say that you do. I believed in so many people that hurt me. I don't want to be disappointed again. So, let's stay in touch and get to know one another. I have so much love to give, but I have to be sure that you want the same things that I want. I want a family and children. I want a husband that will love and protect me. I want to be able to teach the word of God and show people God's love. That's all I want really.

P.S., if you see any spots that look like dried up water on this paper, just know they are tear stains, and I'm sorry about that. They are indeed tears of joy, okay. Please be sure that sister Daisy is very well taken care of. I won't stress and worry; it's all in God's hand. Annabelle finally sat her pen down and stood up. She quickly reread her letter and folded it up and eased it inside of a white envelope, and then she addressed it to him and sealed it up. When she finally laid down, she slept with the letter underneath her pillow, but the whole time she was trying to visualize how life would be with Daniel.

CHAPTER 8

*S*ince Black Girl had been gone, her mother had moved to yet another bad area in Atlanta. When she arrived, she had to take a cab to College Park. Her mother lived in a section eight apartment complex on Godby Road called Sierra Townhomes; the name might sound good, but the area and the complex was like a war zone. Constant gunshots every night. The apartment came with roaches and the windows had duct tape on the cracks. Black Girl mother was in her mid-fifties and ran the streets like she was a teenager; she'd only been home a few days and hadn't seen her yet. Her son was five; he was a handsome young man that loved basketball and the Fortnight online video game. His name was Mason; he had dark smooth skin and curly hair and bright eyes.

Inside of their apartment was a plaid sofa set, a wooden coffee table, and a thirty-two inch TV in the living room. Black Girl was sitting on the sofa while Mason played his game from an old cellphone that he got from the neighbors next door. Black Girl was lost in her own world; she couldn't live like that. She rubbed her hand across her face in total disgust and took a deep breath. But, what really had her angry is that her mother left her son with the lady next door and her son wasn't even enrolled in school yet. *What am I supposed to do?* she asked herself. Then, she stood up and there was a knock at the door. She walked over to it and looked through the peephole and saw a white lady in a black shirt underneath a bulletproof vest and khaki pants. She instantly knew that it was her parole officer. Black Girl opened the door and flashed a smile. "Good morning," Black Girl said.

"Good morning," the lady said; she extended her hand out to Black Girl. "Angel, correct?"

Black Girl nodded and shook her hand. "Yes, ma'am," she said. "Come on in."

The parole officer stepped inside and looked around the living room. The stale odor hit her nose and made her frown; she looked down at the little boy. She bent down next to him. "Hey little fellow, what's your name?"

He looked up at her; then, his eyes went to the gun on her side. He looked back at the phone in his hand without saying anything.

Black Girl closed the door. She turned around. "Mason, don't you here her talking to you?" she raised her voice.

Mason looked up at the lady again. "My name Mason. Are you about to take my mama away again?"

"Hello, Mason. And no, I'm not here to take her away. I'm here to help," she said with a smile. Then, she stood and turned and faced Black Girl. "So, how's it going so far?"

"Pretty good. I have a little adjusting to do, trying to get everything situated around here you know."

She nodded and looked around again. "Why isn't he in school?" she asked.

Black Girl had to think quick. "He has a dentist appointment in thirty minutes; we were on our way to the bus stop actually," she lied smoothly.

"I understand, what about work? Have you found a job yet?"

"Not yet, but I'm on that. God will send me in the right direction. Give me a few days."

"Sure, but you know having a job is mandatory on parole, okay."

"Yes ma'am, I'm very aware," Black Girl said; she straightened up her shoulders to give herself a more energetic look. Then, she said, "I have a few questions."

The parole officer lady folded her arms across her chest. "Okay," was all she said.

"How hard will it be for me to move?"

"It's not hard at all. Just get the new address, call me, and I'll go check it out and, if it's good, you good to go," she said. "Are you plan on moving?"

"Yes, I want my son in a better area; I want him at a better school. I just want better for us as a whole, my son is all I got," she lowered her voice, and then she went on. "And I don't want to lose him to the streets."

The parole lady stood in silence for a moment. She unfolded her arms and slowly began to nod her head. Then, she placed her hand on her shoulder. "I tell you what. I'm not going to place you on a curfew, but I'm trusting you to do the right thing, okay."

Black Girl nodded her. "You got my word."

"Where are looking to move to once you get yourself situated?" the parole officer asked.

"I'm not sure yet, but far away from College Park. Maybe Gwinnett, wherever God see fit for me," she said. Then, her eyes went down to her son; she watched him for a moment and the parole officer's eyes looked down at him also. When her and Black Girl looked back at each other, she reached inside her pocket and pulled out her card. "My number is on the card. Keep me posted, and please try your best to stay out of trouble; this is definitely a high crime area."

"Yes ma'am," she said and took the card. "You just don't know how much I appreciate this. And I'm done with the streets so that part you won't have to worry about." Then, she opened the door; the parole officer walked out. She turned around.

"See you later, Mason," she said.

Mason lifted his head from the phone screen and waved at her. When Black Girl closed the door, she locked it and went back to the sofa and sat down. She dropped her head and stared down at the floor. Then, out of the blue, a fat flying cockroach went zooming across her face; she jumped up and took off her right shoe and killed it on the wall behind the sofa. "I got to get out of here. This ain't gone cut it," she said to herself. Black Girl walked into the kitchen and went and wiped up the roach with a paper towel. "I got to get me some money," she whispered softly as she walked to the sink and washed her hands.

As she did that, she began looking around the kitchen and, for an apartment, it looked worse than a project hallway. Black Girl took a deep breath and looked up toward the ceiling. Then, an idea jumped into her head. She snapped her fingers. "I got to try it." She went into the living room while wiping her hands on the side of her jeans. "Mason, I need to borrow your phone for a few minutes," she said to him.

"But, I'm almost about to finish this stage," he said without looking up at her.

Black Girl politely walked over to him and took the phone from his hands. He gave her an angry look. However, he wouldn't dare fix his mouth to say anything out the way to her; she was looking at him, waiting for him to say something. "I'll give it back to you in a few minutes. If everything goes right, I'll buy you a PlayStation 4 and you can play on your own big TV in your own room."

Mason finally stood up. "I'm going to Demond house next door."

"No, you ain't," Black Girl said; she pointed towards the hallway. "Go in the back."

Mason slowly turned around and, without another word, he went towards the hallway and headed down the hall. When Black Girl saw that he was gone, she looked at the phone and went to Facebook login and typed in the login information that Annabelle had given her for the Sunday School Teacher page. The information was indeed correct. Black Girl looked at the number of people that was following that page and was almost at three million followers. She couldn't believe it; she got on her knees and knelt in front of the sofa and began to pray.

"First of all, I want to thank you, Father God, for bringing me to this point in my life. What I'm about to do will probably be wrong in some people's eyes, but I hope you understand; this situation I'm in right now is worse than being in prison. My mother just abandoned my son and Lord only knows where she is. He's not enrolled in school and I just can't come this far to lose him. I'm not going back to prison. Please protect me, bless and watch over my mama wherever she is. Amen."

She got up off the floor and sat back down on the sofa, and she took a deep breath. Black Girl pressed the Live button on the Facebook page. She took another deep breath and said. "Here goes." She began looking at the small phone screen; the heart emoji began floating up and several followers started commenting.

"Hello."

"Are you the Sunday school teacher?"

"Hello and, no, I'm not the Sunday school teacher. I'm

here to tell ya'll our story once we get enough people on here," Black Girl said while smiling into the phone.

"God is good." Another comment came up.

Black Girl looked at the number of people that was already online watching and it was up to seventy-three thousand. That was indeed a large number of people that was already watching her. She stood up, holding the phone out in front of her. It was over one hundred thousand viewers now.

"First of all, allow me to introduce myself. My name is, Angel. But, I grew up by the nickname Black Girl. I'm actually from Atlanta, Georgia and I still live here now. A few years ago, I went to stay in a shelter, and I left my only son to live with his grand mama. My life wasn't all peaches and cream; I was in the streets doing whatever to survive. Gang lifestyle was my life. Smoking marijuana, popping pain pills, and drinking liquor had become an everyday thing for me. I was a thief, stealing clothes and using stolen credit cards and stuff like that. So, one day while I was in the shelter, I met this beautiful young lady by the name of Annabelle and, when I met her, she was on her knees praying," she paused for a second.

The viewers were growing by the minute. She went on. "I asked her to pray for me because I was going to steal, so my son could have some clothes. She prayed with me, she prayed for me. And, then, we lost contact with one another. Several months later, God brought us back together. Except, when we met back up we were in prison."

She paused and watched the comments flow in.

Look at God.

You have the right name, Angel. So blessed. Another comment appeared.

The comments were coming in by the hundreds and there was no way that she could read them all right now. She started talking again. "It was crazy what we went through.

She needed my help and I needed hers, and we finally connected the way that God wanted us to. When this page was created, Annabelle created it because it was something that God wanted her to do. I'm not sure if ya'll remember when she said that a friend of hers had gotten saved. I was that friend that gave my life to Christ."

Her eyes were beginning to fill with tears now, but that didn't stop her. Black Girl propped the phone on the sofa. Then, she removed her shirt and tossed it to the side and, now, she was standing in front of the camera in her black bra. "I'm not trying to make anybody feel uncomfortable or anything. But, I want to show you guys how real God is. I was stabbed in prison over twenty times after I left the gang life alone and gave my life to Christ. She slowly turned around and allowed everyone to see her bandaged wounds and some of the puncture scars and scrapes.

"They said that I wasn't going to make it. The Devil lied as usual and, not only did I make it, I was paroled out just four days ago and now I'm home. As of now, my living conditions isn't quite like I want it. When I arrived, my mother wasn't here and my five year old son was staying next door with the lady that I don't know. My son hasn't been enrolled in school for whatever reason and I just don't want him raised up like I was raised up. Am I asking for any help? Yes I am, I'm starting a GoFundMe account in a few minutes because I want to get my son out of this poverty stricken neighborhood and I want to make sure that Annabelle has some support as well. As of now, I still study my Bible, I still walk on the path that God has laid for me. If anybody want to write Annabelle Humphrey, please be sure to take this address. It's 2023 Gainesville Highway, Alto Georgia three-zero five one-zero and, like I said, this young lady is nothing less than an Angel sent from God. She helped me get my life together; she's also helped several other women in prison to find Christ, please write her. And until she comes home, I'll probably be running her page for her."

Just then, she was interrupted by her son. "Mama, I'm hungry," Mason said.

She looked down at Mason. Then, she pointed the phone at him. "Say hello to everybody."

Mason smiled. "Hey everybody," he said, waving his tiny hand at the phone as if he was in a high-school parade.

"Well, I got to go fix Mason something to eat. Thank you for listening and God bless you." She logged off. Then, she instantly went to GoFundMe and set up her account and posted the link on the page and also underneath the live video post.

"You want mommy to heat up a can of beef mac and cheese?"

He nodded his head up and down. She went into the kitchen and started fixing his food in the microwave.

CHAPTER 9

*B*y ten o'clock that same night, Black Girl was looking at her GoFundMe account and was impressed that the amount was up to $177,356.00. Her heart started to race; she was nervous as all out doors and her eyes filled with tears within seconds. She dropped the phone and covered her mouth with both of her hands and just shook her head side to side in disbelief. "This can't be real," she said.

Immediately, the Lord spoke to her again. *Behold the fowls of the air: for they sow not, neither do they reap, nor gather into barns; yet your heavenly Father feedeth them. Are ye not much better than they? Matthew 6:26. The word of God always affirmed that He was with her, so it was obvious how any of what was happening possible.*

Black Girl leaped to her feet and danced around the front room, giving praises to God. "God, You are mighty and so good to me, and I thank you for everything."

And they said, Believe on the Lord Jesus Christ, and thou shalt be saved, and thy house. Acts 16:31. The Lord always reminded her of his word.

Black Girl smiled. "Yes! I hear you, Lord, and I will worship you for the rest of my days."

After she caught her breath and calmed down, Black Girl walked into the back room where her son Mason was lying on the twin size mattress that was on the floor. She sat down on the bed next to him; he was sleeping peacefully. She rubbed her hand on the side of his face and, in a low whisper, she said, "Mama is going to get you out of here. Tomorrow, we start our new beginning." She rubbed his face and his head and continued to thank the Lord in silence.

The following morning, Black Girl was up bright and early, that's if she got any sleep at all. It was seven a.m. and she was fully dressed and sitting on the sofa. She logged in to the Sunday School Teacher Facebook page and the first thing that she typed in was: Good morning, God bless everyone that's reading this post. I can't explain to ya'll how grateful that I am. Today, I will start my journey in pursuit of arranging better living quarters for my son and I. And I hope not to bore you guys by walking ya'll all through my process with me. Thanks.

She hit the post button and stood up and went and got Mason up. "Go wash your face and brush your teeth, okay. We going to be leaving in a little while."

Mason woke up from his deep sleep; he rubbed his eyes and stretched. "Where are we going, Mama?" he asked her.

"To a better place than this, Mason. Now, get up and go get ready."

Mason moved the sheet from his body and sat up in bed. When he headed towards the bathroom, Black Girl went back into the living room. She paused for a minute because she didn't know what to do next. She went to Google and researched how to withdraw her money from the GoFundMe account. She looked at the time on the phone and knew that she had almost two hours before the banks opened. The good thing was that she did have a personal checking account at Bank Of America with $33.76 in it. It was still active, and the closest one to her was about five miles. *If I leave now walking, I'll be there in an hour and I can wait until they open.*

Nine a.m. on the dot, Black Girl and Mason were standing at the front door waiting for the bank to open. And when it did, she was led into a private office with a pretty Arabian lady. They talked for the next hour. Black Girl set up a personal account for Annabelle, herself, and Mason and transferred twenty-five thousand into it. She then set up another account for herself and filled out for two credit cards in her name. Another hour had passed and she was trying to get everything in order. Mason was sitting in the chair next to her with the phone in his hand playing a video game.

By the time Black Girl walked out of the bank, it was almost twelve o'clock on that sunny afternoon. From there, she took an Uber to the Sprint store and purchased a brand new iPhone and got Mason one as well. Her next stop was a car lot; she told the Uber driver that he could leave. Her and Mason walked inside of the building. She was greeted by a male salesman that introduced himself as John. He wasn't really that tall; maybe five nine with a medium build, a chiseled face and an even trimmed beard. "Good morning," he said to her. He looked at his watch and realized it was after twelve. "Sorry about that. Good afternoon."

Black Girl smiled. "Good afternoon."

"What can I help you with today?" he asked her.

"I'm not really sure. I want something that will be great on gas, but I need something with some room as well and good on the road," she said.

"Follow me," the guy said. He headed towards the double glass door that she came in. Black Girl followed behind him;

her nylon backpack was on her right shoulder and Mason was right there by her side. When they got outside, an all-white 2016 Mercedes- Benz GLC caught her eye. She went to it. Then, she started walking around it; she looked through the glass. She looked at John the salesman.

"I want to test drive this," she said to him, and then she added, "But first, if it's a lemon, please let me know now. And if you just trying to make a sale, please be straight up with me first."

"Ma'am, I'm standing behind me and my word. Now, if I'm not mistaken, this SUV has about twenty eight thousand miles, never been in an accident or anything," he said while rubbing his hand across the hood.

Black Girl nodded her head up and down. She looked down at Mason; she saw him looking at the SUV also. Then, she asked him, "You like this one, Mason?"

He nodded his head up and down; then, he said in a soft innocent voice, "Yes mama."

She looked back at John. "I want this one."

The following morning, Black Girl drove out to Alpharetta in her new Mercedes with Mason on the passenger side. She found a nice townhouse inside a gated complex; it was a two bedroom, upstairs, and a roomy living room and kitchen downstairs and a two car garage that was optional. She toured the place, and she loved it. Mason would be in a nice elementary school and there was nothing else that she wanted but her friend Annabelle to be released from prison.

For the next few days, she stayed in a Holiday Inn Express on Windward Parkway. She wasn't trying to go back to College Park never. Inside her room, she sat on her bed reading her Bible, while Mason was playing a game on his new phone. Black Girl wasn't a faker; she was dedicated to God and following the steps that she needed to. After she finished reading, she went into the bathroom and took her clothes and stepped into the shower. The water was steaming hot and it beat up against her skin in a smooth like rhythm; she was indeed in need of it because she had been through so much in the last few weeks. Today, she felt like she was in heaven. "Thank you, Father," she said to herself. "Only you know."

I KNOW EVERYONE, Angel. And there is no such thing as right and wrong. Just love everyone, touch people, everyone will not be able to grasp my calling like you did. Everyone will not be able to reach the masses like Annabelle. You still have work to do, but don't move too fast.

* * *

MISS DAISY MAE'S head was completely shaved; she'd been through chemotherapy and she was now back at Daniel's estate being waited on hand and foot by the four nurses that was hired just for her. Daisy Mae had her own bedroom and a king sized bed that was beyond comfortable and came with a remote to adjust to her body movement and temperature. She had a wonderful view through her floor to ceiling window. She walked over to it and just stared out into the sky, the trees, and the front yard, taking in the beautiful scene.

A nurse walked in the room; she was carrying a bowl of fruit in one hand and a bottle of something called Black Seed Oil in the other hand. Daisy Mae looked back at her just as she was sitting everything down on the stand on the side of the bed. "I don't want any more of that oil stuff," she said. "It's just nasty." Her face frowned up at the thought of it going down her throat.

The nurse smiled, then said, "One teaspoon a day keep the doctors away."

"Baby, you can give me the doctors," Daisy Mae said while shaking her head.

"Okay, this time you can take a spoon of raw honey with it to dilute the taste. But, you have to take it."

Daisy Mae poked her lips out and turned back towards the window and stared out; she folded her arms across her chest, and she was stubborn as can be. Then, she said, "I want to talk to Daniel." She had her back to the nurse, never turning around to face her. Then, out the blue, there was a knock from the door. The nurse and Daisy Mae turned around at the same time; Daniel walked in with a smile.

"Good morning ladies," he said. He came all the way in and closed the door behind him.

"Good morning," Daisy Mae said. Her voice was dry, but she was glad to see him. Then, she said, "I'm fine, why do I have to take this black oil?"

He grinned. "The black seed oil. Nigella sativia is all natural. The taste may be a little tart but, trust me, it's good for you. The doctors said he swear by it. I even take it myself." He walked over to the stand where the bottle was at. He twisted the top and grabbed one of the two shiny teaspoons and poured himself some in the spoon. He eased it inside of his mouth and did everything he could not to frown as it went down, but he couldn't help it. "Uggg," he said.

Daisy Mae frowned at the sound he made; then, she said, "See there, that stuff is terrible."

"But… just take it for me, please. I promised the doctors that you would take it. I promised myself and Annabelle that I will take care of you to the best of my ability."

Daisy Mae just shook her head side to side. She moved over towards him, picked up the other spoon, and held it out in front of him. "I'm ready," she said.

Daniel smiled; then, he poured her a spoon. Daisy Mae pinched her nose and eased the spoon in her mouth. She frowned as it went down. Then, she grabbed her bottle of water that was on the nightstand. She removed the top and turned the bottle up; the whole entire time, she was frowning and Daniel was trying to hold his composure to keep from laughing. But, he couldn't; Daisy Mae looked at him. And the expression that was on her face would be asking him: What are you laughing at?

Daniel wiped the smile off his lips. "I'm not laughing at you; it was just the face that you made was so funny to me," he said.

"Yeah, whatever," she responded back to him, and then sat down on the bed and removed her feet from the bedroom slippers that she had on. Daniel bent down and lifted up her feet and helped her get into the bed. "Thank you," was all she said.

"You're welcome," Daniel responded back to her, as he sat down on the bed next to her. "How are you feeling?"

"Pretty good actually."

"Well, I know you ready to get back to Atlanta. And I'm ready to go see, Annabelle." He paused and looked back at the nurse that was still standing there over by the door. Daniel told her that she could leave and he would call her when he needed her. She turned and walked out of the door. He looked back at Daisy Mae. "We've been writing each other letters. I actually told her that I wanted to marry her."

"And what did she say?"

"Well, she didn't say no but, of course, she didn't say yes either." He shrugged his shoulders, as he spoke with sadness.

"Well, Daniel, you did ask her in a letter," Daisy Mae said, then paused for a brief moment. "Everything will happen on God's time. He brought ya'll this far, didn't he?"

He nodded his head, then looked at her. "Yes, he brought us this far. I also told her everything about me and my life."

"Good, I'm sure it's interesting. Cause I know I ain't never seen no rich white man just fall out the sky and want to marry a young pretty black girl that's in prison. I guess it's just something that the Old Spice men do," she laughed.

Daniel laughed with her for a moment. Then, his phone rang from the inside of his pocket. He pulled it out and looked at the screen. It wasn't nothing important, so he stuffed it back in his pocket. "But, before you leave, I want give you a tour of London."

"Ain't interested, I'll see it when Annabelle come home."

"Well, I don't think that will be long. The attorneys we have are good; the first step right now is getting the Appeal in. The judges will grant it. They we're asking for an appeal bond, so at least she'll be able to come home."

"So, you think it's gonna happen just like that?"

"Well, it should, unless you know something that I don't know."

Daisy Mae's shoulders moved lightly. "Well, I know the state of Georgia. But, I know the grace of God, too. So, I'll just pray on that what you are telling me."

"I'm confident that she will be home in the next couple of months. I'm so confident that when we get back to Atlanta, I'm buying her a house there," he said, and then added, "But, I got one problem."

Daisy Mae looked at him; she didn't like the sound of the one problem. "What is it?"

"I want you to stay there with her, with us."

"Oh naw, baby. I got my own house right there in Kirkwood," she said. "And I can't wait to get in it."

"I understand, it'll just make it easier for us, as a family," he paused and took a deep breath. Then, he turned his body around and reached for Daisy Mae's hands. She extended hers, and they held hands. He bowed his head; she did the same.

"Dear Father, combine our strength together; we are sending prayers up for Annabelle to be released on her appeal bond. Bring her out here with us. Also, I'm asking you to remove every ounce and grain of cancer from our mama Daisy Mae right here. This is the direction that you lined me up for, and I can't thank you enough for bringing me so much peace and love into my life. Thank you for allowing me to be the person to help Annabelle and this lady right here in front of me. I only want to be a better man for you, myself, and my family. Amen."

"Amen," Daisy Mae said. She was still gripping his hands; her eyes were still squeezed shut and her head was nodding up and down.

Daniel was looking at her. She was still praying but, it was in silence; she was moving her lips, nearly mumbling here and there. Then, a tear fell down each of her cheeks. Daniel squeezed her hands tighter. "We are blessed, we gonna be alright."

CHAPTER 10

*N*early another month had passed by, and Annabelle and Daniel was there to see Annabelle every visiting opportunity. Today, when he went to visit her, he was dressed in khaki pants, a powder-blue Polo button down shirt, and some Dockers shoes. He was already sitting at the small round table waiting for her, and on the table was two salads, two bottles of water, and a candy bar for himself. He saw the door open near the front of the visitation area, and Annabelle walked through it. They instantly made eye contact. Both smiling, eager to be close to each other. She gave the officer at the front desk her ID card and information and went towards Daniel. He stood up and met her before she could get to the table, and they wrapped their arms around each other and just held each other for a long moment. They kissed. Annabelle started it; it wasn't anything that she was ashamed of, even though she had heard the talk about her and Daniel inside the prison. Some of the other women shared encouraging words and were happy for her but, on the flip side, she heard harsh words and statements like:

Fake Christian.

Kill a black man. Marry the white man.

You a snitch, you work for the Warden.

However, Annabelle was just as strong as they came; those words went in one ear and right out the other one. Most of the women back there that had so much hatred in their hearts didn't have anybody coming to see them, didn't have God in their lives; they were just miserable and everybody across the globe has heard the phrase: Misery loves company. They finally sat down across from each other. Daniel opened his bottle of water. He had a look on his face as something was wrong, and Annabelle noticed it.

"What's the matter?" she asked him.

He turned up his water. When he brought it down, he said, "They denied our appeal on ineffective assist of counsel."

Annabelle's eyes went straight to the floor and it seemed as if all the life had drained out of her. Daniel reached across the table and put his hand underneath her chin. He lifted her head; she was already crying. Then, he said, "But, they granted it on miscarriage of justice."

Her eyebrows bunched together. "What does that mean?" Her eyes were on his now.

"That means we filed several grounds, but the ones that got them looking is that there was one lady on your jury trial that wasn't a legal citizen; she was Spanish and couldn't understand English that good," he said. "The lawyers said we can get an appeal bond. If that happens, or let me say when it happens, you'll be able to come home until they decide if we are going to have a new trial or not."

Annabelle covered her face with her hands. Her heart was throbbing; she knew it was real now. The tears flowed without warning. Daniel held her hands and watched her cry. It was to the point that he had to stand up and hold her;

then, they cried in each other's arms. A few minutes later, a female officer walked over to them and told them that they had to sit down or their visit would be terminated. "Yes, ma'am," was all Annabelle said. She sat down in her chair and wiped her face with some of the brown paper towels. "Oh my God!" she nearly yelled out, but it was still loud enough for the people around her to hear.

"I'm going to go ahead and get our house. But, before I do or say anything else…" He got out of his chair and got down on one knee in front of her. Then, he pulled out the ring that he had to get approved to bring in. He opened the suede lavender box and produced a diamond ring that was four carats and sitting in a mound of platinum. "Will you marry me, Annabelle?"

Annabelle nearly fainted right there; her face was all the way covered now. In between the tears she said, "Yes," without any hesitation whatsoever.

The entire visitation room erupted with claps and cheers from the other women prisoners and visitors. Annabelle couldn't believe it; it was like a dream. Then, she said, "Wait, this isn't a dream, is it?"

Daniel put the ring on her finger and pinched her. "Did you feel that?"

"Yes," she said with a smile.

"When it's from God, it's as real as it could possibly be."

"Thank you, Daniel," she whispered. Then, she said, "I love you."

"I love you too," he said.

When Annabelle walked out of the front door of the county jail where she was convicted, she was greeted by a host of people. First of all, Daniel arrived to pick her up in a stretched limousine; he had Daisy Mae and Black Girl with him. Her team of attorneys were out there in the parking lot as well; they all greeted her with a hug and a smile. Then, there was a news crew there that had been following her case from the beginning. Annabelle was so overwhelmed; she just paused in the middle of the parking lot and dropped to her knees and clasped her hands together, looked up to the pretty blue skies, and said, "Thank you, Lord."

Daniel got down on the ground with her and so did Black Girl. Daisy Mae stood there over them and cried with them. "Won't He do it," Daisy Mae said while patting Annabelle on her back and shoulder.

When they all piled into the limousine, they talked and just had fun together until limousine driver rolled down the front panel window. "Sir, we are almost there," he said.

Daniel pulled out a thin scarf; then, he looked around at everyone. "Well, I haven't told anybody but everybody here about the house," he laughed. Then, he wrapped the scarf around Annabelle's eyes. She knew that he had got a house, but she hadn't never seen it before because they had had so much going on with her coming home.

Black Girl asked her. "What is your favorite color?"

"Pink," she said from behind the blindfold. Her face was full of joy when she responded.

The limousine was pulling into a long driveway on Saddlesprings Drive in Alpharetta Georgia. When the limousine finally came to a halt, Daniel stepped out first. He grabbed Annabelle by her hand and led her down. He guided her right next to him. "Just stand right her for a minute," he said to her.

The driver was at the door. He helped Daisy Mae and Black Girl down, and they stared in pure amazement at the huge estate. Daniel walked Annabelle up to the front of the house in the center of the circular driveway. Then, he removed the scarf from her eyes. Annabelle just stared at it for a moment. She didn't respond to anybody; just continued to stare at it. Then, she finally turned around and looked at

Daniel. "I'm tired of crying, Daniel," she said. Then, she hugged him. "I love it."

"Come on, let's take a look inside." He took her by her hand; they walked up the brick steps that led to the wooden French doors. When Daniel eased the key into the lock, he went into the foyer that was setting the tone with floor being cover in hardwood. There was seven bedrooms all together in the estate; they walked further inside and went into the huge spacious kitchen where Annabelle pictured herself in there cooking. She walked over to the island top and stood on the other side. She looked at Daisy Mae. "Oxtails, rice and gravy on you?" she asked her.

"Oh yes," she said. "But, somebody won't let me eat like I want to," she said playfully and cut her eyes at Daniel.

Daniel laughed. "Well, maybe one unhealthy meal won't hurt," he said.

Then, out of the blue, Annabelle said, "Before I do anything else, go through the rest of the house, eat, or anything. I need to go see, Pastor James."

Daniel shook his head. "Impossible, one of the appeal bond conditions is that we can't have any contact with victim's family whatsoever." And he said that like he meant it.

"What about a phone call then?" she asked.

"Annabelle, if you need me to go deliver a message to him for you, I will do that. Other than that, I'm not going to chance you going back in that prison for something as small as that."

She paused for a minute, thought about it. Then, she said, "I understand." She walked from around the island and went over to Black Girl and put her arm around her neck. "I owe so much to you," she whispered.

Black Girl hugged her. Then, she whispered to her, "You don't owe me anything, Annabelle. If anything, I owe you, sweetheart."

"Well, let's give what we owe to God," Annabelle said. They hugged each other tighter and slightly rocked side to side.

"I hope you know how to swim Annabelle because it's a nice pool out back," Daniel said.

"Hold up," Daisy Mae said. "Where my room at?"

Everybody looked at her at that moment. Then, Daniel said, "I thought you said..."

"Never mind what I said, that was a long time ago anyway. And who gon' cook 'round here?"

Everybody started laughing. Daniel walked Daisy Mae to the guest room that was on the main floor; they walked through the double doors and there was a huge spacious room that was already decorated neatly and fully furnished. They all walked in and there was a wall window that gave them a perfect view of a lake out back. "I'm going to get my stuff," she said.

Black Girl turned to Annabelle. "I put Mason in aftercare today because I knew I wouldn't be home when he got there. But, I got to go get him," she said.

"Baby, go get your baby and do what you got to do," she said and hugged her again.

"The driver will take you to your car, Angel," Daniel said.

"Is he gon' take me to get my stuff also?" Daisy Mae asked.

"We gonna probably get a moving company for your stuff, Mama," Daniel said.

Black Girl had to get to her house to get her car so she could go get her son; she went and gave everyone a hug.

"I want to see you tomorrow, Angel," Annabelle said but, the way she said it, Black Girl felt like something wasn't right.

She nodded her head up and down and then said, "I'll be here," she said. Then, she added. "I'll see you'll tomorrow." After that, she walked out and went straight to the limousine.

The driver held the door open for her and she climbed in when he closed the door. She was in the back seat wondering what Annabelle had on her mind. Either or, something wasn't right.

Back inside the house, Annabelle and Daniel walked through the rest of the house holding hands. They finally got upstairs to the master bedroom; it was spacious. There was a California king sized bed with huge white wooden posts. There was a fireplace to their left by the window with three chairs bunched up around it. She was more than impressed. "I love it," she said. "But, why do I feel like something is missing?"

"I'm not sure, Annabelle." Daniel said. Then, he added, "I just want to make you happy like you make me happy."

They stood in silence for a moment. She looked towards the window; her mind flashed back to when her and Jamal was standing in the window together. She snapped out of that quickly. She didn't want to think about that; she didn't want to think about him. "Maybe I just need to relax and find some inner peace. What room can I turn into the prayer room?" she asked.

Daniel walked her through the house. She found a room in the basement. She was in there for over an hour meditating and talking with God.

CHAPTER 11

The following morning, Annabelle was up at five thirty a.m. No alarm clock went off; her body was just adjusting to waking up at that time of morning. When she stepped out of the bed, she looked at Daniel. He was out cold with the covers pulled up to his neck. She leaned down and kissed him. "Good morning," she whispered.

He turned on his side a little; his eyes were still shut tight. "Good morning," he finally said. Then, he asked, "What time is it?" He began wiping his eyes.

"Five thirty, go back to sleep. I'm going to pray and cook breakfast," she said and slipped her robe on and walked out of the bedroom. Annabelle walked down the stairs, bypassing the main level and went straight down to the basement. There was a theatre room down there, a gym, and kitchen; the private room to the right was the room she called the Prayer Room. She went inside and closed the door. There wasn't any furniture in there. Just wall to wall carpet, no windows, and wood grained finished walls. Annabelle sat in the middle of the floor in Indian style. She put her elbows on her knees and pressed her fingers together and relaxed her mind and sat there with her eyes closed for about fifteen minutes.

When she finally opened them, she took a deep breath and said, "Lord, sometimes I feel lost, regardless of how much I pray to you. Regardless of how many people that I help to find the way, the right way. I mean, with me. I don't care what you need me to do, I'm going to do it. But, I do have something that I need to do, and I'm asking you to watch over my every step as I go. I can't thank you enough for sitting me down and, even more, bringing me home. Does it seem real? No. But, I can just only assume that this is the part that some people be talking about when they say that you will pour blessing into lives so big that they will be passed down to the kids and grandkids. Then, you send me Daniel. I'm not going to get into the story, you already know it. But, in the Bible, Daniel means God is Judge. I believe you know what you are doing. Anyway, I have a little business to handle today."

She stood to her feet, looked up at the ceiling, and pressed her hands together. "All praise to you, Father God." She took another deep breath and walked out of the room and went upstairs. She didn't have a phone and hadn't seen one in the house. But, she needed to call Black Girl, and the only way that she could do it was to go back upstairs and get Daniel's phone. She walked back up to the bedroom; he was still asleep underneath the covers. She saw his phone on the nightstand, resting in the charger. She grabbed it, walked out the room with it, and went downstairs. Annabelle sat at the kitchen table and dialed Black Girl's number. The phone rang four times before she finally answered it.

"Hello," Black Girl said in a groggy tone of voice from the other end.

"Angel," she said. "Sorry to bother you this early."

"What's wrong, Annabelle?" she asked.

"I need you to do me a favor."

"I'm listening," she whispered.

"I have to go see Pastor James." She swallowed hard, didn't know what Black Girl would say from the other end.

The silence sat in the air between the two of them for a long moment. Then, Black Girl finally said, "But why…"

"Because it's eating me alive Angel," she whispered, nearly covering the phone with her hands. "Please understand where I'm coming from."

Black Girl breathed into the phone. "Please don't make me be a part of this. What if he decides to just be hateful and tell the judge that you came looking for him?"

"I don't think he's like that."

"Did he send you one letter while you were in prison? Did he put one dollar on your account?"

"No, he didn't," she responded back.

"And you still want to go?" Black Girl asked.

"If you don't mind."

"Okay, give me an hour, let me get Mason on the bus. Or I'll just take him to school and come and get you."

"Thank you, Angel…"

"I just hope we're making the right decision. I'll see you in a little while," she said and hung up the phone.

Annabelle sat there for the next five minutes; she was thinking how Pastor James would react if he saw her pull up at his church. *Maybe I shouldn't go to the church*, she thought to herself.

She got up, walked upstairs, and placed Daniel's phone back on the nightstand and, when she turned to walk out, Daniel asked, "Is breakfast ready?"

She turned around and smiled at him. "Not yet." Then, she said, "I borrowed your phone to call Angel."

"Okay, look right there in the nightstand on your side, I bought you a phone. I just forgot to give it to you yesterday."

Annabelle walked around to the other side of the bed and opened the drawer and there was a brand new iPhone sitting there. She pulled it out and looked at him. He was looking at her; they both smiled at each other. Then, he rolled over and sat up. "Are you going shopping today?" he asked.

"Yes, I want to," she said.

"Okay, I'm going to get everything situated with the movers for Mama Daisy Mae. I don't want her moving back and forward like that because of her condition. But, it's going to get started today."

"Alright, I'm going to head downstairs." She walked over to him and gave him a kiss. Then, she left and walked downstairs. When she got to the kitchen, she actually had to cook breakfast; it was funny that she hadn't been home a whole twenty-four hours yet, and she was already lying and going towards the wrong direction. When she got to the fridge, her heart was racing just as well as her mind. She tapped the glass on the window and she saw everything that was inside the refrigerator. Then, she heard a door behind her. She turned around and saw Daisy Mae walking towards her. Annabelle wasn't use to her with the shaved head. But, she didn't care, as long as she was there with her.

"Good morning, baby," Daisy Mae said as she wobbled over towards her and gave Annabelle a hug.

"Hey baby," Annabelle responded back to her. Then, she said, "I was just about to cook some breakfast. But, I'm going to be honest, I need your help."

Daisy Mae didn't say one word; she just went over to the refrigerator and opened it. She removed a carton of eggs. There was a box of breakfast sausages to the left; she pulled them out also. Then, she put everything on the granite island top. "Find the grits," she said to Annabelle.

Annabelle went to the pantry to the left and opened the door. Inside were stacks of can food, mostly canned veggies and fruits. She looked up to her right and saw the bag of grits, there were oatmeal as well. She didn't know what Daniel ate, his favorite food, or anything like that. When she grabbed the bag of grits, she walked out and sat them on the island top next to the eggs. "Thank you," Daisy Mae said to her.

"You welcome," Annabelle said; her mind was somewhere else though. She wasn't focused on the breakfast; all she was interested in was making the peace with Pastor James. *Where are you, Angel?* she said to herself. Then, the doorbell chimed.

Annabelle walked out of the kitchen and went towards the front door. When she got to it, she looked through the peep hole and saw Black Girl standing there on the other side of the door. She opened the door. "Hey, come on in," she said to her.

Black Girl walked in; she wasn't happy with Annabelle decision at all. Annabelle felt it as she entered. After all that time of knowing each other, they had never had any issues until then.

Now this.

When Black Girl stepped inside, she turned and looked at Annabelle. "Can we talk before we make this move?" she asked her.

Annabelle closed the door and faced her. "Sure, let's go downstairs to the prayer room," she said. She turned around and they walked downstairs, one behind another. When Annabelle led Black Girl into the prayer room, she closed the door and flipped on the light. Then, they faced each other. Black Girl's arms were folded across her chest. Her eyes were fixed on Annabelle and Annabelle's eyes were fixed on hers. "So, I'll assume that you think I'm making a mistake."

"Honestly, yes," Black Girl said. "You got plenty of time for that. We don't know if we have to go back to court for a new trial; the risk is greater than the reward."

"I'm the reward, my heart hasn't been right in two years," she said and dropped her head for a moment; the entire room was silent.

Black Girl reached out and grabbed her hands. She said to Annabelle, "I understand and, whatever you need me to do, I'm ready." She was shaking her head at the same time.

"Thank you, Angel. We can eat breakfast first. I already told Daniel that we're going shopping, and we are. I just got a stop to make," Annabelle said while staring Black Girl in the eyes.

"I don't have an appetite right now. When we back here and I know you alright, then I can eat."

Annabelle nodded and turned around and walked out of the door. They went around the corner and headed up the stairs; Black Girl was right behind her. In her mind, she didn't feel as Annabelle was making the right choice and that alone was eating her up inside. When they got to the kitchen, Daisy Mae was just pouring the scrambled eggs into the frying pan. And to Annabelle's surprise, Daniel was sitting at the table with his phone pressed up against his face.

"Yes, I understand." His eyes went to Annabelle. He blew her a kiss, then spoke back into the phone. "Perfect. See you then," he ended the call. Then, he said to Annabelle, "That was the attorney. He's five minutes away; you got to sign some papers before you leave."

Annabelle's face relaxed, but she was covering up her feelings. "And it's nothing that we can sign later on this evening?" she asked.

Daniel stood up; he walked over to Annabelle and wrapped his arms around her waist. "It's only going to take a few minutes, Annabelle; why are you in such a hurry?"

Annabelle shrugged her shoulders and just leaned into Daniel's arms and held onto him. "I'm not sure," she whispered to him.

He rubbed her back and slowly rocked side to side, while Black Girl and Daisy Mae were in the kitchen working together.

DING DONG.

"That must be the attorney," Daniel said. "Come to the door with me," he said to Annabelle.

CHAPTER 12

*W*hen Daniel and Annabelle arrived at the front door, Daniel opened it, and just on the other side was a lean dark man; he was dressed in a wrinkled shirt, a pair of denim jeans, and it looked as if he hadn't shaved in a week. Daniel extended his hand out to him, then he said, "Pastor James. Correct?"

He nodded.

Annabelle looked at him closer. Her heart began racing; it felt like it was about to leap from her chest. His eyes shifted to her and they stared at each other for a brief moment. She examined him; he didn't look like the same Pastor James that she'd remember from the church. His eyes showed pain and grief. Something wasn't right.

"Good morning, Annabelle," he said to her. He released Daniel's hand and opened his arms for her, and she hugged him; tears began streaming down her face. Pastor James was trying to hold back his tears, but it was impossible. He began crying as well. Annabelle looked back at Daniel.

"You always arranging stuff," she said to him.

He smiled. Then, he winked his eye at her.

"Come on in, Pastor," she said to him. They all walked inside.

Daniel stood at the door for a moment; he saw the attorney sitting outside in his smoked white Tesla Model S. He waved at Daniel and Daniel waved back. The window came down and he said, "He's good to go; all the paperwork is signed."

Daniel gave him a thumbs up. He closed the door and turned around. Annabelle and Pastor James were standing there in the foyer, waiting for him. He said gently, "I'm going to let you'll go somewhere and talk in private."

Then, Annabelle said. "First, let me introduce you to everyone." She led him straight to the kitchen. He walked in behind her. Daisy Mae was standing over the stove talking to Black Girl.

"See, I'm not supposed to be eating no pancakes but they sho' look and smell good."

"Sister Daisy. Angel," Annabelle said.

They both turned around at the same time. Angel didn't have a clue as to what was going on, but Daisy Mae recognized him instantly. For a moment, they stared at each other; there was so much going on between the both of them emotionally that the energy could be felt in the room. Pastor James walked over to Daisy Mae and stopped just in front of her. Then, she looked at Annabelle and Daniel and said, "Ya'll could've at least let me know we was having company. I would've put my fancy wig on."

Everyone erupted in laughter. She reached out and they hugged; she'd figured if he was here, everything was nearly alright. When they hugged, Pastor James said, "You look just fine, sister Daisy."

"Thank you, baby. It's good to see you," she said. "And may God continue to bless you."

"Thank you so much, thank you so much. Just being in

the same place with ya'll makes me feel that much better," he said. Then, he pulled back from her. He kissed her on the cheek; then, he went to Black Girl. He put his hand out to her. "Good morning, I'm Pastor James."

"Nice to meet you, I'm Angel, a close friend to the family."

ANNABELLE AND PASTOR JAMES separated from the rest of the house. They walked out to the back of the house in the yard; there was a table there with four cushioned chairs. Their view of the lake and the pool was calm and breathtaking. They both took a seat across from one another. Annabelle took a deep breath. "I've been waiting for this day forever and now I'm at a loss for words," she said.

"Well, let me start," he said. "First of all, I forgave you the day that I got the news about my brother."

"That's something that I really needed to hear," she responded back.

"Let me explain something to you, Annabelle. Jamal was my only brother. And I wanted so bad for him to get his life together, not just for me or him or our mother. But, for God. And when I saw the reaction that you had on him, I just knew he was on the right track. Finally, I said. But you know what? God don't make no mistakes."

"God don't make no mistakes," she repeated, and tears were streaming down her face as she looked at him and listened. Then, she said, "I wrote you letters to the church and I never got a response from you or anyone."

"I don't have the church anymore," he said. His voice lowered and he looked out towards the lake and took a deep swallow. When he looked back at her, he shrugged his shoulders. "Things just started going downhill for me after that."

"Downhill, like what happened?" she asked.

He rubbed his hands over his face and took another deep breath. "I got caught up in a scandal."

"At the church?" she asked with concern.

"At the church," he said; his eyes went down to the table and then he looked back up at her. "I was in a relationship with a woman that was a member of the church. I mean, she wasn't married, I wasn't married, and I didn't really see anything wrong with it. I wasn't dealing with any other women or anything like that, but what happened was the lady was there trying to get under me because she apparently thought that I was a rich preacher with a lot of assets." He took another deep breath. "When I realized what she was after, I call myself trying to cut her off. And it wasn't that easy; she had all these crazy family members that kept sending threats to me. Then, they were coming up to the church catching me in the parking lot, talking about the girl was pregnant and what not. So, now everybody in the church was dragging my name through the mud; the lady was tagging me on Facebook with her sonogram pictures," he paused. "I just stepped down as the pastor; it was too much stress for me. But, the best part about it, the baby wasn't mines."

"That was God, he has something greater for you," Annabelle said. "So, what are you doing now?"

"Just preaching from a podcast, under another name. But, it's not authentic because I'm hiding the real me."

Annabelle sat and listened. All this time, she thought everything was all peaches and cream with the pastor. Now, the situation had turned to something that she wasn't expecting. Then, she said, "Your problem isn't a problem, it's just a minor issue. So bad I know that I needed to apologize to you, your mother, the members of the church. And I still want to. So right here, right now, I sincerely apologize to you and your family for what happened. However, my situation was justified and I've paid for my mistakes."

"Your apology is accepted, Annabelle," Pastor James said. His head was going up and down.

Annabelle smiled and wiped tears away at the same time. "I just came home yesterday. I'm out on an appeal bond, but I just couldn't stomach being out here without making my peace with you first."

"I don't even know how to thank you."

"Thank me for what?" she asked.

"Annabelle, you are the only person that I've talked to about this situation besides God. See, I know your heart, I knew you wasn't like the rest. And once again, God don't make no mistakes. We all know that."

For the next hour, Annabelle and Pastor James talked about everything. They discussed the past, the present, and even future endeavors. Before he left, Annabelle asked him and the entire house to come downstairs to the prayer room and everyone prayed over everyone. And Annabelle's last words were, "A family that prays together, stays together. Amen."

Later that night, Annabelle and Daniel were lying in bed together. Daniel had his laptop opened. He was doing some work and she didn't want to disturb him, but she had something on her chest that she really needed to get off. She turned over on her side towards him and propped her head in the palm of her hand. "Daniel," she said softly.

Daniel looked over at her. He saved whatever he was doing on his computer and closed it down. "Yes," he responded and slightly turned towards her.

"I love you," she said to him.

"I love you, too," he said back to her. He moved down so their eyes could be leveled with one another.

"Did you know that Pastor James stepped down from being the pastor at that church?"

"No, I didn't. And actually, the first day that I ever went to see Mama Daisy, I asked her to take me over there because I wanted to meet him. She didn't think it was a good idea, so I left it alone."

"Now, I have a question. How do you feel about us having our own church?"

Daniel allowed that question to sink in for a moment. Then, he simply said. "Is that what you want to do?"

"Yes. And I know we still have this retrial thing to go through, but I'm more than sure everything will fall in place."

"And you want pastor James to be the face?" he said to her.

"Right, and Angel. And me and sister Daisy will be the Sunday school teachers."

Daniel smiled. "I guess you got it all figured out," he said to her.

Annabelle laughed. She leaned in and kissed him but, this time, their tongues twirled around one another. That was their first night making love to one another.

CHAPTER 13

s the weeks passed, life was moving in the right direction for everyone. That morning, Annabelle and Black Girl had taken Daisy Mae downtown to see her Oncologist to take some more blood test and PET-scan. And when she walked out of the doctor office and saw Annabelle, she had a big smile on her face. "He said the PET scan didn't detect any cancer at all, baby." She had on her wig, but it looked good on her. Daisy Mae was now losing weight because Daniel made sure that she had her own personal trainer that was coming to the house making sure that she was eating healthy and working out. Her main thing was walking on the treadmill at a causal pace and she looked forward to it every day. Annabelle stood up and hugged her, and Black Girl did the same thing. They had one big group hug and they laughed and cheered for a moment and, of course, they praised God together.

They left the doctor's office and all climbed in Black Girl's SUV. When they got on the road, Annabelle turned on her phone and connected it to the car radio. She played a song called My God Is Awesome by Charles Jenkins.

"My God is awesome," she began singing along with the song.

Daisy Mae and Black Girl started singing along with her. "He's great. He's mighty… He's mighty."

"Oh, I love that song," Daisy Mae said and continued to sing along. She was just moving her head side to side and clapping her hands from the backseat.

Annabelle was looking out the window as they rode in silence for the next few minutes. Then, she looked over at Black Girl. "Can you take me over to Red Oak Road?"

"Red Oak Road? Let me think where that's at. I can put it in the GPS real quick." She looked at her phone and pulled it up. "It's only ten minutes away from here," she said.

"It's over by Flat Shoals Road, what's over there?" Black Girl asked.

"Daniel wants us to come over there," she said. Then, she looked at her phone again. She looked in the back seat at Daisy Mae and saw her looking out of the window. "How are you feeling back there?"

"I'm fine baby," she said. "Just… blessed."

Annabelle smiled at her; she turned back around and rode in silence. She was looking out the window as they passed the moving traffic. She was lost in her own world, thinking about Daniel and their future; she was also thinking about the case. The country town that she was sentenced in wanted to take her to trial again, even though her attorneys wanted a guilty plea, so she wouldn't have to go back to prison. She allowed all of that to sink in and, by the time she came back to reality, she noticed Black Girl was slowing down. Annabelle looked over at her but she didn't say anything. Then, Black Girl asked, "What's the address?"

"Sixty two seventy," she said. She began looking on the street; they rode further up until she saw the old model church that she was looking for. Annabelle pointed over to

the church on Black Girl side of the road. "That's our desti-
nation," she said. She was now sitting up in her seat looking
at the church as they were pulling into the empty parking lot.
Annabelle saw Daniel holding a rolled up sheet of paper that
appeared to be the blueprint for the church. When Black Girl
parked, she looked at Annabelle.

"Don't tell me this," she said.

"Yep, I hope you ready," Annabelle said. She opened the
door and stepped out. When she closed the door, she went to
the back door and opened it for Daisy Mae.

"Who church?" Daisy Mae said as she was stepping down
from the back seat.

"Ours," Annabelle said. She closed the door and started
walking towards Daniel. The church was an older building
that was made of red bricks on one side and stucco on the
other side. When she got next to Daniel, they kissed with a
peck and she asked. "Where is Pastor James?" she asked him.

"He's inside and he's excited."

Black Girl walked up; she was looking at the church in
disbelief. She walked off by herself and went around the side
of the building. She was only looking and examining the
scene. She turned around and walked back over to Annabelle
and Daniel. Miss Daisy Mae was now standing there with
them. Pastor James walked out the front door and came and
hugged everyone except Daniel and said hello to all of them.
"Now that the cat is out of the bag," Annabelle said. "This is
the family church. It's gonna take a little work, but I think we
can get it to where we want it to be," she paused and looked
at Pastor James. "Can you and Angel run this church
together?"

Black Girl looked closely at Annabelle, she wasn't
prepared for this. She looked at Pastor James; they stared at
one another for a brief moment. "Are you with me?" Pastor
James asked her.

She shrugged her shoulder. "Whatever I need to do, I'm with you."

He looked back at Annabelle. "We can handle it."

"Great," she said and looked at Daisy Mae. "I need a Sunday school teacher," she said to her.

"Baby, I done got a little too old now."

"I'll help you, but I want it just like it was when we started before," Annabelle said to her.

Daisy Mae stood in silence for a moment; she turned her head and looked at the building again. She knew she didn't have the energy to wrestle with kids anymore but, by the grace of God, she knew she had a purpose. She slowly turned and looked at Daniel and Annabelle at the same time. "I'm honored to take the position," she said and went over and hugged Annabelle. She said to her, "I just don't know what else to say about y'all."

"We love you, Mama," Daniel said. He walked over and hugged her also.

They walked on the inside of the church; Daniel was leading the way. "Now," he said and went on. "We are definitely going to upgrade the church; I just don't want to overdo it. Like, should we go big?" he asked.

"Big as in?" Pastor James asked.

"I was thinking tear out the ceiling, put more seats up top. We may bring out a really huge crowd. Annabelle already has millions of followers just on Facebook alone. If we tell the world our story, people will start coming from all over the world."

"Millions of followers?" Pastor James looked at Annabelle with a questioning look over his face. "How did that happen?"

"It's a long story," Annabelle said.

"Well, let's go big," he said.

Pastor James looked at Black Girl; he didn't say anything.

She noticed that he was just looking, so she said, "What's wrong?"

He shrugged his shoulder a little. "Since we'll be working together, we need to sit down and put a plan together."

"Just let me know when you free," Black Girl said.

She nodded her head and just said a simple, "Ok."

"Well," Annabelle said and looked at the time on the face on her iPhone. "We got to get sis... Mama home." She was smiling at Daisy Mae. "Mama just sounds better than sister," she said to her.

"I like it. I couldn't have a better daughter," she said.

"Six months, I want to have our church up and ready to go," Daniel said. They talked for a few more minutes and they parted ways. Annabelle, Daniel and Daisy Mae all rode home together, and Black Girl left alone. Pastor James drove off in a F-150 pickup truck and jumped on eighty-five and rode in silence for the next thirty minutes, until he got off on an exit and made a few more turns. He found himself pulling into a huge graveyard on Westview Drive. The truck was moving through the uneven dirt road, but he pulled over on the side where his brother was buried at. Pastor James parked and got out. He looked around, scanning the many different tombstones. He walked up to Jamal's gravesite and knelt down at the head of the stone and placed his hand on the gray stone.

"Hey man," he said. "I just wanted to let you know that I'll always love you, and also to let you know that I did come all the way apart after your death, but I'm getting myself back on track. It's funny that you just never know who God will send to you for help. But, I'm not complaining. God doesn't make mistakes." He leaned down and kissed the top of the tombstone, and then he patted it softly. "I love you brother and, now, I'm moving on." He slowly turned and walked back to his truck.

* * *

THE FOLLOWING DAY, Daniel and Pastor James met up at the church in the parking lot. They both got out at the same time and met up at the rear of Pastor James' truck. They shook hands. "How's it going?" Daniel asked him.

"I'm blessed, that's about all that I can say as of now," he responded back. Then, he asked Daniel. "How's everything going with you?"

Daniel released his hand and, with a smile on his face, he said. "Life couldn't be greater." He pulled out a notepad that he had tucked away in the small part of his back and turned towards Pastor James. "So, what I figured is. We can use this church, for let's say two years. Now, I know you are probably going to bring some of your members over, either or. I really feel like we're going to need a mega church."

"A mega church?" He scratched his head, as if he was going a little too big for him. "I'm not sure about that, not at this location anyway."

Daniel studied the paper again without saying anything. He looked back up at Pastor James. "Well, we'll expand this one to hold at least five thousand members."

"That's a good number, at least starting off," Pastor James said confidently.

"Anything else that we might need?"

"When I checked the inside yesterday, I noticed the kitchen could be expanded and the daycare room will need some work."

Daniel pulled out his pen and began writing on the paper, jotting down a few things that would be important in the near future. He looked back up at Pastor James. "Annabelle brought it to my attention that we may need some security as well."

Pastor James thought about the situation that occurred at the last place; his eyes went to Daniel and he said, "Yes."

"I mean, I want you to be as comfortable as possible," he said to him.

"I have a question for you," Pastor James said to Daniel.

"Okay."

"She didn't tell you?"

Pastor James shook his head. "I never asked her. I mean, all this happened so fast that we just never had a chance to get around to it. I don't even really know much about Angel either," he said to Daniel.

"I got an idea," he said. "Let's take a break from everything today. We going to go out, just the four of us. Is that alright with you?"

Pastor James curled up his lips and nodded his head at the same time. "I'm free whenever."

"Great." He turned around and went to his rental car; he opened the passenger side door and he grabbed his iPhone and walked back over to Pastor James. He pulled up Annabelle's number and called her. She answered on the third ring. "Hey Baby," he said.

"Hello," Annabelle said from the other end.

"Do you think we can arrange a dinner date tonight with Pastor James here and Angel, just the four of us?"

"I don't see why not, Angel will have to get a sitter for Mason. Other than that, I don't see why not," she said.

"Okay, well, we're taking off for the rest of the day. I'll see you in a maybe an hour."

"So, are we eating at home or are we going out to a restaurant?"

"Your choice," he said.

"Okay, I'll get it handled on my end," she said. Then, the call ended.

Daniel eased his phone in his pocket and looked at Pastor

James. "Everything is a go," he said. "I'm going to arrange us a limo."

"A limo?" Pastor James repeated.

Daniel placed his hand on Pastor James' shoulder. He looked at him and said, "I'm just use to certain things, and I'm in love. So, bear with me if it seems like I'm over doing it a little."

Pastor James nodded. "I understand," he said, and then he asked him, "Where are you from?"

"London."

"Like the real London, Eiffel Tower London?" Pastor James asked.

"That's it," he said with a smile. "Now, let's get ready to enjoy the day."

CHAPTER 14

They arrived at Cabernet Steakhouse on Windward Parkway at 6:45 p.m. The limousine driver pulled up in the front of the restaurant. The valet guy was already waiting for them; he opened the rear door. Daniel stepped out first; he wasn't over-dressed at all. Just a simple blazer jacket, denim jeans, and a pair of hard bottom dress shoes. He greeted the valet guy with a slight bow of the head. Then, he reached inside and took Annabelle's hand. She stepped out in a cream colored blouse, linen pants, and two-inch heels. Her makeup was light, but it had her beauty enhanced even more.

Black Girl stepped out next, and she actually had to purchase something earlier today for the dinner. She was dressed in a multi-color Versace dress and matching heels. Even though she was more of a blue jeans and sneaker type of female, she actually loved how she looked today. Now Pastor James, on the other hand, had taste when it came to dressing, most of the Pastors did anyway. When he stepped out, he was in a fitted black shirt, cream colored pants, and black Versace shoes with the gold Medusa head on the top.

His beard was trimmed, and his hair was tight. When they entered the restaurant, they were escorted to a huge booth that was designed to sit six.

Once they were all seated, they were handed menus. But, before they made an order, the four of them joined hands and they bowed their heads in prayer. "Dear Father, first we all want to say thank you for joining us together," Pastor James said. "Thank you for giving me a second chance, thank you for bringing these beautiful people into my life. I ask of you to continue to bless Annabelle and Daniel on their new journey in life that they are about to be on for the rest of their lives. I want to thank you for this young lady named Angel that's right here next to me, many blessings for her and her son. We also want to say thank you for giving sister Daisy Mae another chance. Everybody know that cancer is real. So, we want to continue to keep her in our prayers; we pray for great health and to keep us in good spirit as a whole. In Jesus name we pray. Amen."

"Amen," the three of them said in unison.

When they all released hands, Black Girl looked at him. "Thank you," she said to him.

Pastor James looked her in her eyes; he stared at her for a moment. "I need to be thanking you," he said.

She smiled. "Thanking me for..."

"Just peace and happiness," he said to her. Then, he looked at the menu, hoping that he wasn't making a mistake. "I don't know what to order from here," he said to everyone.

Over the next two hours, they all sat and talked amongst each other. Pastor James was overwhelmed by the connection between the three of them, and it was so strong that he felt like he didn't fit. But, God had the final say so on if he was meant to be with them or not. And by the way things were looking, this was his family now. Inside the restaurant, there was a small dance floor in the bar section. Pastor James looked at Black Girl. "Do you want to dance?"

She looked at him; then, she looked at Annabelle for the right answer. Annabelle said with a smile, "Don't look at me."

She looked back at Pastor James. "Why not?"

Pastor James looked over at Daniel and Annabelle and started easing out of the booth. "We'll be back in a few," he said and stood up. Then, he reached for Black Girl's hand.

She took his hand, and he helped her out of the booth. The whole time, she was blushing as she stood up. When they got to the dance floor, Pastor James went to the DJ booth and whispered to the DJ and slipped him a folded twenty dollar bill, and then Luther Vandross' voice came through the speakers: If This World Were Mine.

When they came together chest to chest, Black Girl kind of relaxed in his arms; they swayed side to side and just dance in silence with their eyes closed. Pastor James whispered to her. "Why does this all seems like a fairytale story to me?"

She didn't respond right then but, in the next fifteen seconds, she took a deep breath and said, "I think sometimes people can go through so much pain in life that when it's time for the healing process, it seems like that."

Pastor James breathed into the crook of her neck. "Do you feel like that also?"

"Every day that I wake up, I feel it. I mean, from all that I've been through from the streets and in prison, getting my life right with God, I haven't quite grasped it all yet."

He opened his eyes and looked at her and, at that moment, Kem came on: I Can't Stop Loving You.

"I love that song," she said with a smile. "Did you request that?"

"Yes, I did," he said. Then, they got quiet again and just enjoyed the song, the dance, and the rest of the night.

"Pastor James."

"Just call me James, Angel. And yes."

"Yes what? You don't even know what I was about to say."

"Well, I thought you were going to ask me if I were single."

"No, I was going to say that I had to pee, and these heels were hurting my feet," she said and laughed lightly.

"Are you serious?" He smiled.

"No, I'm joking," she said back to him.

Pastor James couldn't do nothing but laugh at that. He looked at her and shook his head. "You are very funny," he said to her.

"Well, the first thing I had to see was if you could take a joke," she responded back.

"Clearly!" Pastor James said. He pulled back from her and grabbed her hands. "I just want to be happy."

"We got something in common then." Then, she said, "But I do have to go, so I can get my son."

"I understand." They walked from the dance floor and, when they got back to the booth where Annabelle and Daniel was sitting, they were close and holding hands. When they looked up and saw them, they both started smiling at the same time.

"We're back," Pastor James said to the both of them at the same time.

Annabelle looked at Black Girl and she saw a glow on her face that she hadn't never seen before. In return, that made her smile even brighter. "Look like you guys had a lot of fun," she said.

"We did," Black Girl said. She looked over at Pastor James; his glow and happiness matched hers and, with that alone, it felt like magic between the both of them.

* * *

"WHY YOU JUST SITTIN' there lookin' at me?" Daisy Mae said to Daniel while she was sitting in the chair on the rear deck, shelling Lima beans and enjoying the nice spring weather.

"I was just trying to see what you were doing out here," he said, looking at her hands and the beans.

"I'm shellin' the lima beans. You ain't never seen nobody shell beans before?"

He shook his head and said, "Not where I'm from."

"Well, sit down, let me show how to shell 'em," she ordered.

"Are you serious? I got to go down to the church." He gave a confused look.

"Boy, sit yo' behind down, it don't take long," Daisy Mae said, nearly in a demanding tone of voice that left Daniel with no option.

Daniel pulled up a chair next to her. He studied how she was popping open the hulls and tossing them in a bucket and dropping the beans in the pan on her lap. He reached over and grabbed one and followed her directions, and he got it. "See how easy that was," she said. Then, she handed him the pan that she had on her lap; he took it and looked at her as she stood up.

"Where are you going?" he asked her.

"I got to take me a break. I'm cooking a big Sunday dinner tomorrow. Lima beans, ham, fried chicken, candied yams, sweet potato pie. I might let you taste my pork chops smothered in gravy and with that white rice. Ump," she said and closed her eyes and moved her mouth, as if she could taste the food right now.

Daniel was looking up at her as she was talking, and he noticed how happy she was just talking about it. "Okay, Mama. Go take you a break; I'll handle it," he said to her.

Daisy Mae slowly turned around and, with her side to side wobble, she made her way into the house. When she closed the door, Daniel pulled out his phone and sent a text message to Annabelle and asked her to come outside to the rear deck.

She responded back. Okay.

Three minutes later, Annabelle was walking through the glass door. When she got outside, she immediately started laughing at the sight of Daniel sitting in the chair shelling lima beans. "You got to be kidding me right now," she said and pulled out her iPhone and started recording him. "Okay," she said. "So, here we have my fiancé all the way from London, Paris who probably don't even know what lima beans are, and now he's way over here in Atlanta Georgia learning the country way to prepare dinner."

Daniel laughed and kept on shelling the beans as she went over to him and gave him a kiss, Annabelle sat down next to him and started helping him. "She caught you up I see," she said to him.

"Yes. And I have to get to this church to meet with the contractors." He gave her the pan of beans and stood up. He kissed her again and asked, "Are you sure ya'll will be alright while I'm gone?"

"Yes." She sat the beans down and stood up with him. Then, they walked inside the house and she walked him outside to the front of the house. When he pulled out of the driveway, she turned around and went back inside the house. She went across the floor to Daisy Mae's room and knocked on the door before entering. When she didn't answer, she turned the knob and pushed the door opened. She saw Daisy Mae lying in her bed. Annabelle walked up to the side of her bed to check on her. She was on her side; her eyes were open.

"Ya'll got them beans shelled already?" she asked.

"Woman, don't scare me like that. Why are you laying in the bed like that? How do you feel?" Annabelle said to her and sat down on the bed next to her.

"I feel fine. my stomach just turning, so I came and laid down."

Annabelle laid down with her. Daisy Mae moved over a little, so she could get comfortable. "I'm going to get you some Ginger Ale. That will make your stomach feel a little better."

"What's going on with you? It something on your mind," Daisy Mae said.

Annabelle was lying on her back looking up at the ceiling. "I'm not even sure really. I mean, I'm home. I feel so blessed and grateful to have you in my life. Do you really know how good this makes me feel?"

"Baby, when God created you, he already knew what he had planned for you. None of this wasn't a stroke of luck," Daisy Mae said. "You got everything that's supposed to be yours. I love you more than you can imagine. You have a great select of people around you. You just make sho' you be a good wife to that man."

She rubbed the side of her face. "I will, and that's a promise." Then, she said. "But, how do you really feel about Pastor James and this church situation?" Annabelle asked.

Daisy Mae paused for a second. "It's not 'bout how I feel, baby. That's just the power of the Lord. And honestly, Pastor James has always been a great man. But, nobody on Earth is perfect. We God's children; even though we may be grown, we still make mistakes. Pastor James needs ya'll just as much as you need him."

Annabelle got quiet. She just laid still for a few minutes, and all they heard was each other breathing. Her eyes on the ceiling, she was lost in her thoughts for a second. Then, she said. "I really want to have our wedding at our church, nothing too fancy though. I mean, if this case wasn't hanging over my head, I would rather get married in London." She laughed a little. "I remember Daniel sent me a letter and said that you didn't want to go sightseeing over there until I came home. Well, I'm home. And you doing fine. Are you ready?" Annabelle was smiling and just allowing her imagination to run wild. When Daisy Mae didn't respond, she turned her head towards her. Daisy Mae's eyes were closed. "Mama," she said.

Daisy Mae didn't move; Annabelle put her hand on the side of her face. She didn't flinch. Annabelle just laid there and stared at her until tears fell down her cheek. She hugged her stiff body. "I love you," she whispered.

CHAPTER 15

*P*astor James stood at the podium at his old church, in front of a crowd of over two hundred people that came out to show respect for sister Daisy Mae. Before he said one word, he had to wipe his own eyes as he looked down at her casket that was right there in front of him. He took a deep breath; his eyes scanned the sea of people that was looking at him. The cries from babies were bouncing off of the walls of the church. Old ladies were weeping; most of them knew her from many years ago and some of them knew her from the church. The next thing that Pastor James did was reach inside his inside jacket pocket and pull out a folded sheet of paper. He adjusted the microphone, cleared his throat, and began reading from the paper that was before him.

"My hate letter to you. First of all, I hate your guts and everything about you. Ever since you've came into my life, it's been a total disaster for me, my family, and millions of other families across the world will cosign this letter and agree with me. So, you call yourself Cancer? And you just go around destroying lives like it's all good. Well, let me tell you something; you took my mother away from me many years ago and you were the reason I had to go through a living hell. I even turned my back on God, just because I didn't know that you were the problem the whole time. I'm sure you don't know how it feels to not have one, but two mothers taken away because of you. Why do you choose to play games with us? Acting like you're no longer there and then coming back, sneaking in the bodies. It hurt, damnit. Don't you understand that it hurts? Don't you? But, never the less, I'll be here to fight you for however long God allows me to. I'll fight for all the women and men that could no longer fight for themselves. And you can take that to bank with you. Sister Daisy Mae was a dear friend of mine; we taught the kids in the Sunday school teacher class right here in this same church. She was the only person that stood by me when everyone else turned their back on me. And that alone made her a world class champion in my life. You can never stop a person like that. So, just know, you've crossed me one too many times and I have ZERO respect for you. And this is a letter that will never end." Pastor James looked up from the piece of paper that he was reading from; he looked out into the sea of people and asked. "How many of you have lost a friend or family member to this so called disease called Cancer?"

Several hands went up in the air, then claps and women's voices floated through the air. Some were screaming, "Praise the Lord!"

Others were saying, "Amen. God is good."

Pastor James looked out into the crowd and he saw Annabelle there on the front row; she was dressed in black with a veil down over her face. Daniel was sitting next to her with his arm around her neck. Then, he said. "God saw sister Daisy getting tired." he took a long deep breath. Then, he went on. "But, you know the best thing about it all. I had the pleasure of being with her the last few weeks before she gained her wings."

A tear fell from his eye. He bowed his head and began praying. "Dear Lord, please help us all to deal with this loss of our love one. Help us know that you are near to us to help us place our torn hearts back together. You are the only source of our comfort. We have to survive this pain and continue to grow and move forward. Remind us oh Lord that with your help, we can get through whatever that comes into our lives. We ask for strength when we are weak and peace when we are hurting. In Jesus name, we ask these things. Amen," he said and raised his head.

"You may view the body now," he said. He turned around and nodded his head at the choir. They all rose to their feet at the same time; the organ began playing and they began singing one of her favorite songs: My God is Awesome. The people began standing; they formed a line and started walking up towards the casket. Annabelle and Daniel was nearly in the front of the line; he had his arm around her for comfort. But, Annabelle didn't want to be held and she freed herself from him. When she got to the casket, she looked down at Daisy Mae. She was in her all white dress, her eyes were closed, and she looked so peaceful. Annabelle was lost for words. She had so many plans for them, so much love that she wanted to give and now she was gone. Her mind flashed back to when they were in the hospital. One of her most memorable moments.

"Well, if it's not a problem, I'll stay tonight and as many nights as you'd like until you're released." She reached down and grabbed Daisy Mae's hand and, in a joking manner, she said, "Now, I don't want your daughter coming up in here trying to put a beat down on me."

"No honey, all she wanted is to know if I was dead yet, so she could get some money from the insurance policy. When she came

in, I pretended to be asleep. I overheard her fussing with them nurses. Then, she had the nerve to ask the nurse to hook her up with some Percocet pain pills, promising her that she would make sure she cut her in on the profits. But, I know better. Even if the nurse was fool enough to fall for that bunch of bull, that heffa would have run up out of here faster than an Olympic track star to take them herself."

Annabelle chuckled a little bit because from the looks and reeking scent that Pearl gave off, she doubted she sold any drugs that came into her possession. She took a seat and just sat there listening and shaking her head at the same time to some of the stories Daisy Mae had shared with her about her daughter. Their chit-chats were interrupted by a light tap on the door. The same doctor from earlier entered Daisy Mae's room and, when he saw Annabelle, he smiled at her.

"Hey, glad you made it back," he said to her.

Annabelle flashed him a smile. "I'm glad to be back doctor. I had to check on our patient."

The doctor turned his attention to Daisy Mae. "How are you feeling?" he asked her, genuinely concerned.

"I'm doing better doctor and I'm really ready to go home. Can I leave today?"

The doctor smiled. "Not today Miss Carter. We want to keep you at least forty- eight hours. I can't just let you up and leave like that and you're not well enough so, in a couple of days, we'll see how you're doing."

"But, I feel well doc," Daisy Mae replied. "And I want me some Ox tails, rice, cabbage, cornbread, and gravy."

Annabelle was still standing there smiling at the memories of Daisy Mae being her witty self. Daniel placed his arm around her neck and pulled her close to him. "But, why did you have to leave me?" she questioned in a whisper.

"Baby, all I wanted to do was to see you out of that prison;

you have a long life ahead of you. Live it like you suppose to. Just keep our God first. I'll be watching you."

Annabelle didn't seemed surprise by hearing Daisy Mae's voice. She leaned down and kissed her on her forehead. She turned around and saw several faces that she remembered from the church; some of them were looking at her, in hopes that she would say something to them. But, Annabelle was on a different path now and, when she started walking up the aisle with Daniel, she didn't bother to look back. Black Girl was still in the pews; Mason was sitting next to her. Annabelle stopped and leaned down and whispered, "I love you. I'll see you later, okay."

Black Girl nodded her head and hugged her. "I love you, too," she whispered.

Annabelle walked off, and Daniel patted her on her shoulder as he followed behind Annabelle. When they got outside in front of the church, Annabelle's heart felt as if it was about to leap out of her chest. She kept moving towards the limousine; she was far ahead of Daniel and he called her name, "Annabelle!" He was almost jogging now. He ran and caught up with her and grabbed her arm and spun her around to him.

When she faced him, she couldn't help herself, and she broke down in tears. "It's just messed up, Daniel." She cried in his arms; he held her close and tried his best to comfort her.

"I know baby. Go ahead and let it out," he whispered. He looked over at the limo driver and nodded his head at him to alert him to open the rear door for them.

He did.

Daniel moved Annabelle over towards the rear door of the limousine; she went without any hesitation. When they got into the rear of the limousine, the driver closed the door and Annabelle just leaned on Daniel's shoulder for comfort.

Her eyes were puffy from the tears and she was soaking his shirt. "So, you don't want to go to the burial ground?"

She didn't respond; she only shook her head. He pressed the button for the partition to come down. Then, he said to the driver, "You can take us home." He pressed the button and the window went back up; the limousine pulled out of the parking and they rode in silence for a long period of time. Annabelle was curled up next to him like a baby. She hooked her arm around his, then said to him, "I just can't believe that the doctor told her that it wasn't in her blood."

Daniel didn't respond; he really didn't know what to say to it. All of this was new to him and just as hard. Daisy Mae had grown on him also. He looked outside and just stared out in the daylight from behind the limo windows; his hand was massaging Annabelle's shoulder. "I'm not sure," he finally said to her. Then, he added, "However, I do know that I'm not going to allow you to lose it. I'm not going to allow you to be depressed by no means necessary."

"And I don't want that feeling anymore," her voice was low, nearly a mere whisper. After that, the silence sat in and they rode all the way home without sharing a word amongst each other.

CHAPTER 16

*A*nnabelle had an off and on switch inside of her mind. And as of now, it was off; she was in a slump, just like she was when her mother died. It had been two days now since Daisy Mae had been buried and she hadn't eaten anything but a bite from a turkey sandwich that Daniel had fixed her. Even their conversation was short between the both of them. Daniel knew what she was going through because she'd mentioned it to him in one of the letters that she written to him when she was still in prison.

Today, she was sitting in her prayer room in the center of the floor; her Bible was on her lap, and she was reading from Philippians 4:13. "I can do all things through him who strengthens me," she said.

Then, from the outside of the door, Daniel knocked on it. "Can I come in and pray with you?" he asked.

Annabelle looked up at the door, stared at it for a few seconds. "I just need some time alone, Daniel," she said, and she looked back down at the Bible.

"I've gave you enough time alone, Annabelle," he said through the door. "Come to the door."

Annabelle got up. She held her page in place with her finger and walked to the door. She put her face to the crack, but she didn't unlock it. "I'm here," she said.

On the other side of the door, Daniel was standing there with his Bible in his hand; he was leaning up against the door. "If you choose not to let me in, I understand, Annabelle. But, I didn't come this far to let you down. And if I have to sleep on the outside of this door just to know we're close to one another, I will." He took a deep breath. His shoulder was pressed against the door and he slowly allowed his body to ease down to the floor. His back was pressed up against the door; he opened his Bible. He said through the door. "Listen at me real quick, I'm about to read something to you." He moved his index finger down to Proverbs and read to her. "Trust in the Lord with all your heart and lean not into your own understanding. In all your ways, acknowledge Him and He shall direct your path." He stopped and said to her. 'That's a verse that you recited to me one day when I came to visit you."

"I remember that," she said from inside the room. Then, she said. "And I remember when you recited me Joshua one nine. 'Be strong and courageous. Do not be frightened, and do not be dismayed, for the Lord your God is with you wherever you go.'"

Daniel smiled. "Yes, that was the day you were mad about something that happened," he said. "But, before I left, we were the strongest together, just like we are now."

Inside the prayer room, Annabelle was also sitting on the floor with her back pressed against the door. "Are you sure you want to marry me, Daniel? It seems like I can't handle pressure that easy, like look at me. I'm stressed and it feel as if I'm about to lose my mind all over again."

"Annabelle, if you lose your mind, I'll give you mines. If

you lose anything and I have it, it's yours. God brought me to you to help you for times like this. Am I sure do I want to marry you? Not only do I want to marry you, but I want us to be together for the rest of our lives. Whatever you have to go through, we will go through it together." Daniel swallowed. His eyes turned red and tears began to fall down his cheeks and small drops landed on the open pages of his Bible.

Daniel's words made Annabelle's heart crush. She wiped her tears from eyes also and all she could do was shake her head. She was looking down at the floor for a second and the tears were just dropping on her Bible. Then, she said, "I don't understand why it seems like I always fail people."

"You don't fail people," he said from the other side. "But, you can't control what God wants. How many times have we said that God don't make mistakes?"

"Several times," she said.

"Open the door Annabelle and let me in," Daniel said.

Annabelle closed her Bible. Then, without hesitation, she stood to her feet and unlocked the door. When she opened it, Daniel was still sitting on the floor crying; his hands were trembling like he was in freezing weather. Annabelle looked down at him. "Come on," she said to him.

Daniel stood up. He tried to get himself together. He couldn't do anything else but hug her. Annabelle wrapped her arms around him, and she then realized that this was all real and God's plan.

* * *

IT WAS 6:09 A.M. the following morning when Daniel's phone rang and woke him from his sleep. He reached on the nightstand and looked at the name and number that was splashed across the screen. It was their attorney. He swiped the green answer button and pulled it up to his face. "Good morning," Daniel said.

"Good morning, Daniel," the attorney said from the other end. "We have a court date."

Daniel eyes rolled to the top of his head. "When?"

"You not going to believe this, but it's in the morning."

"Why such short notice?"

"Because I've arranged for a plea deal."

Daniel sat up quickly and shouted, "A plea deal?"

Annabelle woke up at the sound of his voice and looked over at him. "What's wrong baby?" she asked and rubbed his arm.

"Trust me on this one, Daniel," he said. Then, he added. "This is what I do for a living."

"Yeah. I see you bright and early." He hung up in his face. Daniel sat his phone on the bed next to him and ran his fingers through his hair; he looked over at Annabelle. "Our first court date is in the morning."

"It must not be too good by the way you sound," she said to him. She sat up in the bed with a concerned look in her eyes.

"He said something about a plea deal, but he didn't say nothing else but trust him." He wrapped her up in his arms.

"We can only trust in God, baby," Annabelle said.

* * *

THE NEXT MORNING, the slick attorney Eugene Wolfe was waiting in the lobby of the courtroom building. He was dressed in a tailored fit gray suit, sitting on a wooden bench with his legs crossed. When Daniel entered the door, Annabelle was walking with him. He stood to his feet and extended his hand out to Daniel. They shook hands quickly, and he and Annabelle shook hands even quicker.

"Good morning," he said.

"I definitely hope it's one," Daniel said. He folded his arms across his chest.

Annabelle nudged him and said, "Good morning Mr. Wolfe."

Wolfe turned around and reached inside his briefcase and removed a Manila envelope from it. He sat the briefcase on the wooden bench and opened the envelope. When he revealed the paperwork for them, it was a plea negotiation for two years. When Daniel and Annabelle read it, they both looked up at him at the same time. "So, you asking me to take two years and go back to prison?" Annabelle asked him.

"Honestly, they wanted to go to trial," he said.

"Well, let's go," Annabelle said to him harshly.

Daniel smashed his fist into the palm of his hand and yelled at the attorney in French. "I paid you all of this money and this all you can do! You're fired today!" He walked right pass him and headed for the doors that led to the courtroom. Daniel was angry; his eyes were bloodshot red. When he entered the courtroom, he didn't see anybody. It was completely empty. He stood there breathing heavy through his nose, looking from left to right. When he placed his hands on his waist, he heard the door open from behind him. He turned around and saw Annabelle standing there; the attorney walked in behind her. "Where can I find the prosecutor?" Daniel asked the attorney.

Wolfe walked around Annabelle and went to Daniel. "Listen. Daniel-" he started.

"I don't want to talk to you anymore. Just point me in the direction of the prosecutor. We are not taking no plea; she don't want it and I don't want it either."

Annabelle sat down on the back pew of the court room.

She dropped her head down in her hands; this was too much pain for her right now and her head had started to hurt. Gratefully, the doors opened behind them and in walked a tall, lean white guy dressed in a navy blue suit, a white shirt, and a blue pinstriped tie. He carried a briefcase in his right hand. He stopped when he saw Wolfe standing there. "Hey, how's it going this morning?" he said. He looked at Daniel because he felt that something was wrong by the way that he was looking.

"Are you the prosecutor for the Annabelle Humphrey case?" Daniel asked him.

"Yes, I am." He extended his hand out to Daniel. "I'm David Meyer."

"Nice to meet you, Mr. Meyer." He shook his hand, then pointed over at Annabelle who still had her head down and face buried in her hands. "This is Annabelle, my soon to be wife. And from my understanding, you're offering us a plea for two years."

"Yes, I am," he said.

"Okay, we're not interested in taking it," Daniel said.

The prosecutor looked over at Wolfe. "I thought you-"

"He don't have any say so over this case as of right now. We'll be hiring another attorney today. So, if there is anything you want to say, you can say it to me."

David Meyer stared at Daniel briefly. "I don't really think you understand what you're saying here. This judge is ready to start trial today. He will be ready to pick the jury today."

Daniel just looked at him. Annabelle got up and walked over and stood next to him; she grabbed Daniel by his arm. "Can I speak with you for a second?" she said to him.

Daniel looked at Annabelle. He walked over to the side, just a few feet away from Wolfe and David Meyer. When they got far enough from them, she said to Daniel. "I'm going to take the plea," she said.

"No, Annabelle," he said.

"What did we just say about God doesn't make mistakes?" she said to him.

Daniel threw up his hands and turned and faced the two Devils that were looking at him.

CHAPTER 17

Thirty minutes later, people were filing in place in the courtroom. The prosecutor was standing at the wooden table to the left side of the courtroom; he had his Mac Book Pro open and he was writing up the official paperwork. He had his conviction and that was all that mattered to him. On the right side of the courtroom, Attorney Wolfe was sitting at the other wooden table. Annabelle was sitting next to him; her heart was hurting so bad on the inside and the only thing that was going through her mind was the nightmares of going back to prison. The bailiff was standing to the right side of her with his hands folded and, it seemed as if he was looking directly at her. She looked at his gun, the pepper spray, the Taser, his handcuffs, his badge, his shirt was brown, and his pants were khaki. He would probably be the one that took her away the minute she would say that she was guilty. She turned around; Daniel was sitting directly behind her. She smiled at him. "We're going to be alright," she said to him.

He nodded his head at her but, the whole entire time, he

was praying a silent prayer for her. Out of the blue, the bailiff said, "All rise."

Everyone in the courtroom stood to their feet. The Judge entered from the left side and climbed the steps, draped in his black robe. He was an older white man with a bald spot in the top of his head and he had wire framed glasses on his face. When he got in front of the bench, he leaned into the microphone. "You may be seated." He sat down and looked around at everyone in the courtroom one face at a time. When he looked down at his paperwork, he scanned it for a moment.

Then, out of nowhere, the rear doors of the courtroom opened. Pastor James walked in; he held the door open, and he was holding his mother's arm. She was walking with a metal walker; she was slightly bent at the waist and was dressed in a colorful dress. She also had a flower pinned in her hair. Black Girl was following close behind her holding her leather handbag. Pastor James and his mother walked up the center aisle of the courtroom, and it seemed as if everyone was looking at them. Pastor James helped his mother to her seat in the front row; she sat down and Black Girl sat down next to her. Pastor James went to the table where the prosecutor was sitting and he was already looking at him. He stood up and smiled. "I'm glad you could make it," he said.

"I am too. But, here's the situation. My mother wants to speak with you or either the Judge."

He squinted. "Concerning?"

"She wants to tell the truth about the last DA that was on the case, on how he made us lie to get a conviction against Annabelle Humphrey," Pastor James said.

David Meyer suddenly froze; his eyes were locked in on Pastor James for a long moment. He cleared his throat and wiped his face because he knew it was true. "Hold on for a second," he said. He cut his eyes over to the victim's mother; she was leaning up talking with Annabelle and Attorney Wolfe. That wasn't a good sign at all right now. He looked at the Judge and raised his hand. "Your Honor, may I approach the bench?" he asked.

The Judge waved him up. He walked up to the bench and they talked for a few minutes. He looked back at Attorney Wolfe and waved him up as well. Wolfe got up and quickly walked up to the judge and stood next to David Meyer. "What's going on?" he asked, as if he didn't already know. After they finished talking, Attorney Wolfe walked back to the defendant table and sat down and looked at Annabelle. "They throwing the whole case out," he said to her.

Daniel leaned up closer. "What did you just say?" he asked him.

"It's a wrap. The judge is about to dismiss the entire case," he said with confidence in voice.

Annabelle took a deep breath and then just broke down crying. Then, out of the blue, the Judge said, "Case dismissed." He stood up and exited the courtroom from the side. Daniel stood up and went to Annabelle and hugged her while she cried. Pastor James went and joined in and so did Black Girl. Then, Black Girl yelled, "See, that's what my God do!"

Annabelle pulled herself from the crowd. She looked at Pastor James' mother; her name was Agnes Wright. The old lady stood up, using her walker to brace herself. She outstretched her arm just as Annabelle was coming to her. When they hugged, Annabelle couldn't say anything but that she was sorry and thank you.

"You just keep doing God's work baby," she said, as she cried with her.

Pastor James walked up to them and he whispered in her ear, "I got another surprise for you."

Annabelle looked at him. Her eyes were filled with tears, but her heart was filled with joy. When they all gathered together, they walked outside. When they got into the parking lot of the courthouse, there were over two hundred people out there all holding hands. They were all from the church and from the Sunday School Teacher Facebook page. Black Girl made a post and asked everyone to pray for Annabelle, and some of the local followers in Georgia came out to support her that morning. When they saw Annabelle walk out the glass doors, they all began clapping. When Annabelle saw that, she just covered her face and, in a low whisper, she said, "Oh, my God."

"We love you, Annabelle! The Sunday School Teacher!" one lady shouted into the crowd.

Annabelle walked down the steps. She went up to the people that were out there waiting to meet her and, for the next hour, she hugged and took pictures with many people as possible until the police cleared the parking lot and made everyone leave. That day, Annabelle hadn't experienced anything like that in her life.

* * *

WHEN THEY GOT HOME, it was four o'clock in the evening, Daniel and Annabelle pulled up in the driveway of their estate, and Pastor James and Black Girl were riding together behind them. He took his mother home just a little over an hour ago and the four of them were on relax mode for the rest of the day. When they got inside the house and got comfortable, Daniel looked around at everybody and said. "This calls for a celebration." He looked at his watch, then at Black Girl. "Are you able to leave the country?" he asked her.

She thought for second. "I don't see why not. I only had three months on parole. I'm free to travel."

"Great." He looked at Annabelle. "Where do you want to go first?"

She shrugged her shoulders and, with a precious smile on her face, she replied, "I want to go to London."

Daniel pointed at Pastor James and Black Girl. "Will you guys come with us?" he asked.

"I don't have the funds right now to travel like that," Pastor James said.

"I only asked will you'll come with us."

"Yes," he said.

"I will have to bring Mason," Black Girl said.

"That's fine," Daniel said. And with that being said, they got prepared to leave the country.

CHAPTER 18

he skyline in Paris is beautiful, Annabelle thought to herself as they strolled the streets. The Eiffel Tower was always a main attraction for the city. Annabelle and Black Girl took pictures with their phones. They laughed and talked with and enjoyed their outing. Annabelle and Black Girl was the best of friends and it didn't seem it was going to end anytime soon. From where they were walking, Daniel and Pastor James could see them from their hotel room balcony. Cars were passing by and the horns were blaring at some point or another. The temperature was wonderful, just at or around seventy five degrees that night. Annabelle was dressed in shorts, a Be-Be tee shirt, and a pair of comfortable Nikes. She looked at Black Girl. "So, how's it going with you and Pastor James so far?" she asked.

Black Girl just smiled at her. "All I can say is that I've never been this happy in my life, and Mason loves him," she said. "I guess I can say as long as my baby is happy, I'm happy."

Annabelle nodded her head and they walked a few more steps; it seemed as if they were step for step with one another. "Do you know I've never had a friend like you in my whole entire life?"

Black Girl paused; she turned and looked at Annabelle. "Thanks and, clearly, I've never met anyone as kind, loving, and good hearted as you, Annabelle," she said. "Not only are you my best friend, but I love you like a sister I never had before."

"Don't gas me up now," they laughed.

"Girl, I'm serious, and you a perfect match maker."

"I didn't have anything to do with that," Annabelle pointed and said to her with a smile displayed all over her face. They started walking again. Annabelle had her hands behind her back and Black Girl was just moving with the flow. Black Girl asked her. "So, when are you getting married?"

"Daniel wants to wait until the church is finished, so we can get married there. But, if it was up to me, we could get married today. Right here in Paris."

"Now that would be nice, it's so peaceful over here," Black Girl said. Then, there was a long silence again.

"What about you?" Annabelle asked.

"What about me?"

"When are ya'll getting married?"

"Where did that come from Annabelle?" Black Girl said.

"I mean, when people are happy together, I thought that would be the next step, you happy. He happy. Daniel and I are happy for you. Sounds like a great idea," Annabelle said to her. She had a smile on her face, but it was a serious for the cause and what the matter was at hand. Annabelle knew that her friend was in need to wanting to be happy and she felt that it was her place to help her out with any situation that she could.

Upstairs out on the terrace, Daniel and Pastor James sat and enjoyed the views. They sat around a glass and marble table, sipped on red wine for the occasion and they chatted. Every now and then, Pastor James would peep inside through the double door to check on Mason; he was inside playing as usual on his phone. When he looked back at Daniel, he answered his question. "Yes, I am going to marry her. I mean, I'm going to ask her first and, hopefully, she'll say yes."

"You should propose here in London. I know the perfect place, very romantic," Daniel said. He was more excited than Pastor James it seemed like.

Pastor James picked up his champagne glass and took a sip from it; the red wine went down smoothly. He looked at Daniel and, just when he was about to say he didn't have any money for a ring, Daniel reached in his pocket and pulled out a small velvet box and sat it on the table in front of him. "It's nothing too fancy, I bought this one when I purchased the one for Annabelle. This one is great, just in a yellow gold setting."

Pastor James picked up the box and flipped it open; the diamonds were sparkling, VVS grade for sure. He couldn't believe what he was seeing or believing at the moment. When he looked back up at Daniel, he said. "Man, this is awesome."

"Nah man. God is awesome, this is what he wants for you. And I really want to see you win; it's not always about the money. I grew up in money, but that didn't make me happy. Now, don't get me wrong; it's no fun being broke either, but what I'm getting at is the foundation and having the right people in your life. Annabelle wanted this church for you, I want it for you. God wants it for you. And the same thing that goes for your family situation," he paused and studied Pastor James for a long moment.

Then, out of the blue, Pastor James stood up and walked to the balcony. He looked down and saw Annabelle and

Black Girl just below them walking, talking and laughing, so he yelled down. "Angel!"

Black Girl and Annabelle both looked up at the same time. They were just standing there looking up at him. Pastor James yelled down at her. "Will you marry me?"

Black Girl stood silent for a moment. Annabelle was right there next to her and, when it seemed as if it was taking her too long to respond, she nudged her. "Say something," she whispered. "Don't just have the man standing there looking crazy."

"Under one condition!" Black Girl shouted back.

"And what's that?" Pastor James shouted back down at her.

"Just to allow me to be the best wife that I can be." She smiled and opened her arms out wide.

"Well, if that's all you want. You got it."

"And that's a big ole yes," she said happily.

"Okay, stay right there; I'm on the way down. Don't move," he said and disappeared away from her sight.

Annabelle and Black Girl stood there for a moment. There were several people waiting for him to come down as well; they were just random people that were walking with shopping bags. Other couples were holding hands and waiting for the big surprise. Black Girl looked at Annabelle and said, "I'm so nervous right now."

"Me too," Annabelle said. She reached out and squeezed her friend's hands, just as Pastor James was coming through the automatic lobby doors of the hotel. When he got up to her, he stopped just in front of her and got down on one knee and took her hand. He eased the platinum and diamond ring on her finger and looked her in her eyes as he stood up.

"Thank you, and I won't let you down." He hugged her, and they cried together. All the people that were standing around watching began clapping and cheering for them.

CHAPTER 19

ONE MONTH LATER
PARIS

There had been a small change of plans. Annabelle didn't want to get married at the church; instead, she asked Daniel if they could have a double wedding there in Paris. And, of course, he said yes; the idea was perfect. Pastor James loved the idea and so did Black Girl. So, their private double wedding only had one guest, Mason, and they were witnesses for each other. There were crew members of the yacht but no other friends or family. They'd been married for three days now and they were just enjoying life. The yacht that they were on was called Excellence; it was long and white and they cruised the Atlantic Ocean enjoying the views of some of the monumental landscapes of Paris such as Notre-Dame and the Statue Of Liberty and the night lights were breathtaking. Daniel and Annabelle were on the upper deck. She was at the rail, and he was holding her from behind as they looked out into the sea surrounded by gleaming brass and varnished mahogany just lost in thought for a long moment. Then, Pastor James walked up; he was holding Black Girl's hand. They were dressed in all white linen; the men wore pants and shirts and the ladies wore their white linen dresses. When the four of them got up there together, Pastor James said, "I'm sorry to bother you guys."

Daniel and Annabelle both turned around at the same time; they looked at Pastor James and Black Girl, hoping that nothing was wrong. Pastor James reached his hand out for Annabelle and Black Girl reached her hand out for Daniel, and they all formed a circle. "Just a quick prayer for us," he said. They all closed their eyes and lowered their heads at the same time. Pastor James started off. "Dear Father, only you could've made this all happen. When I was at my lowest point in my life, you brought me out and gave me this, turning total strangers into love ones and best friends. Some days I question myself and ask you do I really deserve this? But, then I can hear your voice in my ears, in my head, telling me yes. This is meant for you. I want to say thank you for blessing me with my beautiful wife, Angel, that says the only problem she has with me is that I snore a little too loud. But, other than that, she is the most grateful, understanding, and loving woman that a man can ask for. And for this beautiful couple that's standing here with us, I ask you to continue to pour your blessings unto their lives. If anybody deserves it, it's them and I plan on being here to watch them receive it. Amen," he finally said.

Annabelle said, "Before we call it a night good Lord, I also want to say thank you for everything that you allowed me to go through and protecting me as I went through it. At some points and time period in my life, I felt like giving up, but you would always come through during your busy day and say keep going, keep the faith Annabelle. Many days and nights, Angel and I sat in that prison trying to vision a better life for us and what would we do once we were out. We all want to thank you together as a family and as one. Because even when someone is in the eye of the storm, you can pull them through if they believe in you. If they trust in you and just have a little bit of faith in you. And in Lord Jesus name we pray. Amen."

"Amen," they all said in unison together. Annabelle realized that her set back was nothing compared to her come back and God rewarded her tenfold. She sincerely knew that God was with her every step of the way, and she'd never stop giving him the glory for her life, even through her worse moments. "Amen," Annabelle said again and put her hand in his, and they lived a life of bliss from that day forward.

THE END

ANOTHER NOTE FROM THE AUTHOR

First of all, I want to say THANK YOU for taking your time out to read this story with me. Secondly, I really struggled with a few things while writing this second part: one is that I never knew the inside history of cancer until I started doing my research while trying to produce this book. I read so many stories online about it and it really had me in my feelings to the point where I wanted to try to find an article that said it was really a cure. Like, I'm not sure what to say but to send a prayer up to everyone that has to go through it as a victim and a family of the person. It's real and its millions of people that are affected by it. I pray for everyone that has lost a family member to it and that God will continue to hold you and keep you strong. Another thing is that when I created the lady Daisy Mae Carter I had my late auntie in mind whose name was Daisy Mae Colbert. She was my mother's older and only sister, and she was also the Sunday School Teacher at the church called Williams Memorial CME. She died while I was still in prison on September

4, 2009. It wasn't cancer, but a blood clot that was the cause of her death. Moreover, at that time I'd already been in prison for ten years. I never got a chance to say anything to her before she departed, so I'm dedicating this book to her. And I know her, and my mother are in heaven probably arguing and fussing with one another as usual, but even with that I'm sure they are very proud of me with my writing career; additionally, the way that I turned my life around. I'm impressed with the results.

Now, allow me to share something personal with you all. I grew up in a single parent home, the youngest of five. Yes, the baby, but I went through a lot of mental pain as a child. Firstly, I was born and raised in a poverty-stricken neighborhood that was surrounded by crime. There were many nights that we were cold, but I was never hungry. This isn't a sob story about me or anything. These unfavorable conditions made it challenging for me to cope with certain things. One of the worst conditions I endured growing up is being raised without Father. As a child you really don't have much of a choice unless your mother finds a man that could handle the responsibility. However, in my case, it never happened. I used to get clowned when I was younger because my mama used to be a heavy drinker. Most of the other guys in my neighborhood knew things about me that I didn't such as who my real Father was and secrets about my Mother that I had to deal with in comedy sessions in my neighborhood. Yeah, so, there were a multitude of things going on with me at the age of ten. Lights out, water off, just to name a few. Nonetheless, I will always remember when my Mama use to tell me, "Baby, you are the man of this house."

Maybe that made me feel good, but I was confused because I was still a kid. When my Mama fell ill and could no longer work, I felt like I had no other choice but to turn to the streets. I was twelve years old at this time. Her words of "being the man of the house" compelled me to try to bring something to the table. Of course, I still had a personal agenda against everyone that picked on me about my Mama and who was and who wasn't my Father. Consequently, I decided to do something about being broke and not having any water to take a bath in. Thus, the streets raised me, and it taught me a lot about life. One thing for sure is that it can make a person depressed and mentally unstable. It's several Mothers that are reading this letter right now: that can relate to my situation, relate to my Mother situation, Annabelle's situation, Daisy Mae's situation and other real-life situations. In 1990, I was sixteen years old and my life was the streets. I never had a chance to go to a prom, a high-school graduation, or even a chance to take a picture in the hallways of Josey High School like most of my peers. Not that I didn't want to, but I just lived a different type of life at that age. The only thing that was my focus: to get rich and to get my Mama out of that raggedy house that we lived in. These were my goals, but it wasn't that easy because I wasn't working a real job. The streets were my life, and bad as I wanted a regular life I couldn't stop doing what I was doing. In November of 1990, I became a Father. Two weeks later, I went to the Youth Detention Center and was gone two years. Basically, I wasn't any better than my own Father. When I came home I may have seen my daughter twice before I went to prison to do another year or two. I just couldn't seem to get it right. Pressure, money, and fame is what I was focused on in the life. Also, I was dealing with my Mama and her having dementia. I guess that kind of made me go deeper into depression because her problems were always my problems. Heavy drugs and alcohol was my savior, at least that what I thought anyway. In February of 1995, I received a call telling me that my Mama was in the hospital. I went up there and joined the rest of my family that were present as well.

Looking at my Mama in that hospital bed just took all the energy out of me. I can still remember what she said when I was younger. "Baby, don't let nobody put me no nursing home."

"You ain't going to no home." I always used to say to her, and I always knew that that was one of her fears.

When I grabbed her hand in that hospital bed I told her that I almost got her home remolded and by the time she gets out of here it would be ready, red bricks, bay windows, new kitchen and everything all in the hood. Then a few minutes later she was gone. The Angels just came and took her hand right out mine. At that point I'm not sure how my life was supposed to go, but it was something that I didn't take very well. Pain, hurt, anger issues, depression, my life had become a living hell. But see, in the streets you have a certain image to uphold. If the streets see your weakness, they will take it right from you. After my Mama was buried, I went harder in the streets for the next couple of years until I had another daughter with my longtime girlfriend. Now I was tired of the street life and ready to settle down. I left Augusta and moved to Greensboro, North Carolina with my girl and our daughter while she was still in college. Still to this day, I love that city. I wasn't paranoid, I didn't have to carry a gun, I could take my girls to the park and walk my dogs. That was what my life was turning into. I was trying to get myself together and on top of that, I had a wonderful woman that was helping me achieve it as well. Once again, the streets made one last phone call to me. Still to this day, I wish I wouldn't have never answered that phone. When I answered the phone, it sounded like the Devil was saying, "Hey my friend, I got a nice life sentence waiting for you."

As you all know, I took the offer and left everything behind: my kids, my fiancé and everything else that I had behind to fend for themselves.

However, once you get your life right with God you can have anything you want and your past life slowly starts to fade away. As I type these last words I can honestly say that I am home, blessed, happy and I have my family back.

SINCERELY YOURS, Jarvis Hardwick AKA Cole Hart